Letters to my Paper Lover

by

Fleur Soignon

AUGUR PRESS

British Library Cataloguing in Publication Data.
A catalogue record for this book is available from the
British Library.

ISBN 0-9549551-1-0

First published 2005 by
Augur Press
Delf House,
52, Penicuik Road,
Roslin,
Midlothian. EH25 9LH
United Kingdom

Printed by Antony Rowe Ltd

Letters to my Paper Lover

With thanks to Fay

Chapter One

Annette stared through the window, with unfocussed eyes. She was aware of the rain running down the outside of the glass, and of the wet greyness outside. It was November. The trees had long since lost their leaves, and appeared content in their denuded form. In some ways she loved this time of year; its darkness brought with it quieter times. Busy people were beginning to concentrate on their Christmas preparations. Let them do that, she thought to herself; they are not bothering me. She was content for now to be closing down and drawing into herself, like the vegetation outside. After all, there was plenty to think about, plenty to reflect upon. It felt as if her life needed her to take time to reassess it, before deciding where next to reach out.

Her work as a teacher at the local college meant that she had good breaks between terms; but being a committed and thorough person, she spent much of her own time gathering extra material for the courses she taught. There was always more subject matter she could include, and she liked to be someone who had more at her fingertips than was strictly required. She knew that this would give extra depth to her teaching, and she believed it would inspire the students, many of whom had dropped out of school in their mid-teens through lack of appropriate stimulation. Although she had to fulfil the requirements of a syllabus, there were frequent opportunities to extend it. It gave her much satisfaction to see her students come alive in response to her enthusiasm.

With biology as her central subject, the possibilities were endless. The difficulty was to limit what she could teach to fit the time available. There were many occasions when her class would keep her back long after the arranged sessions had finished, to ply her with question after question about medicine, ecology, and social issues such as food hygiene and diet.

Satisfying and fulfilling though her working life was, she had become aware that there was something missing. She felt an indefinable emptiness inside herself; and if she tried to concentrate on it, it dissolved into something even more nebulous. Always it eluded her. This was frustrating, but until now she had accepted it, and had assumed that whatever it was would become clearer to her, given time. But today, for some reason, she felt an angry impatience with it. This surprised her, and she decided to spend this day, Saturday, trying to find out more about it.

She went to the mirror that hung in the hallway of her flat, and looked at herself. She saw a woman of medium height and build, with fair hair that reached down to her shoulders. When she had dressed this morning, she had chosen her favourite comfortable clothes – a loose-fitting amber-coloured shirt, a chunky knitted jacket of autumn shades, and a pair of dark brown denim trousers. I don't look bad for my age, she said to herself. Forty-three years old. She was proud of her teeth, and of the fact that her skin had vitality that could be lost by the time a woman was in her forties.

Satisfied with what she saw, she returned to her study and resumed her vigil at the window. I moved to this flat almost twelve years ago, she reminded herself. Her face crumpled a little as she thought about what happened after that move. Her parents had bought a place in a sheltered housing scheme, and they had helped her buy her flat from the proceeds of their home. All of that had proceeded smoothly, and had worked out well for everyone. But the following winter, her mother died of pneumonia during a bad outbreak of flu, and her father slowly wasted away after that. She had been so concerned for them, and so busy looking after them, that she hardly noticed that Brian was contacting her less and less. He had been her partner for several years, and had been a central part of her life. But not many months after her father's funeral, which had been less than a year after her mother's death, he had told her, bluntly, that he was seeing someone else, and that was that.

She wondered again why she had not felt more upset. After all they had been together for more than five years, and had been talking about buying a home to share.

She liked her flat. It was in a stone-built tenement block. The proportions of the rooms were to her liking, and she had exactly what she needed – a large kitchen, a larger sitting room, two bedrooms, a study and a bathroom. The kitchen and the sitting room looked out on the street that ran in front of the block, and the other rooms looked out to the back. Being two floors up, she was above the noise of the street, and she had a good view out across the city from all her windows. She felt very lucky. Her neighbours, although largely keeping to themselves, were friendly, and were helpful when needed. They would exchange an occasional cup of tea with each other, and they kept in touch about issues that concerned their flats. It was always pleasant to meet one of them on the stairway and pass the time of day.

She had chosen the decoration for each room very carefully, and she delighted in walking from room to room, noting the changes in colour and lighting. She preferred subtle pastel shades on the walls, but chose curtains with striking patterns.

Over the years she had lived here she had collected a few unusual lamps, which she used to good effect in her bedroom and in the sitting room. Her favourite was beside her bed. It was a simple design made from a dark metal. She wasn't sure which metal it was, but had been greatly attracted to the dark grey colour of it. The base of the lamp was like the body of a swan, and from it came three individual necks, the heads of which were the lights – candle bulbs, of course.

Brian... he came back into her thoughts. Not only had they talked of buying a home together, but also they had spoken of the family they hoped to have. A tear slid down her cheek. She did not notice it until it reached her lips, where she tasted its salt. Soon afterwards another tear joined it.

She found herself walking through the hall to the sitting room, where she folded up into her armchair, and began to sob. Through her mind flashed image after image of her life with Brian.

Chapter Two

She had first met Brian on a field trip when she was at secondary school. His class arrived at the same study centre, and she had felt drawn to him straight away. Every evening she could sense him looking at her across the dining area, and her cheeks would burn with embarrassment. She talked to her best friend, Steph, about her feelings, and Steph had cut short any further deliberations by engineering a meeting between them. She had simply gone across to Brian, asked him his name, said she had a friend who wanted to meet him, and that was that.

Brian and she had got on like a house on fire. Every evening they sat and chatted their free time away. There was never any need to think of things to talk about. The only problem was that there was never enough time. The days flew past. Each day she threw herself into the course work, looking forward to the evening when, once she had finished her assignment, she had time with him. The others were always around of course, and that was all part of her pleasure and delight. All through her young life she had enjoyed company and companionship, and when Brian came along, it seemed quite natural to her that their conversations should take place in a group. It did not occur to her to think of seeking privacy.

It transpired that Brian lived with his family in a North Yorkshire town not far from where she lived with her parents, so after the course had finished and everyone went home again, they were able to meet at weekends. Everything seemed so easy and straightforward that she never questioned it in her mind. Sometimes they met at his home, and sometimes at hers. Sometimes they went out walking with their friends, and sometimes they would go to see a film. Annette had enjoyed introducing him to more of her friends, and she met a number of his as well.

Annette was an only child, whereas Brian had a brother, Paul, who was about ten years older. Being so much older, Paul seemed a rather distant character to Annette. He was not unfriendly, but his life was elsewhere.

But one day, Brian told her that his family was moving abroad. His father had a prestigious job to go to in Dubai; and in six months' time Brian had gone. They wrote to each other of course, but it wasn't the same. The gaps between writing became longer, and then their writing ceased altogether. By that time, she was nearly eighteen and about to go to college. She threw herself into her new life and made new friends.

Brian had been her first boyfriend, and her first lover. They had never gone quite the whole way, but they had done everything else; and she had felt totally committed to him. And of course, as far as the fantasies of her young mind could conjure, they *had* gone the whole way.

She remembered the first day of the new magic in her life, when they were out on the moors together, searching beneath the heather for bryophytes. She had seen something unusual, and had looked up to attract his attention. That had been the first time. They had kissed, and then she had leaned back into the springy heather. He lay on her and their bodies seemed to explode.

Walking back to the bus afterwards had seemed terribly difficult. Her legs had felt very wobbly and her head felt muddled, although in the most pleasing way imaginable. Parting had been confusing. Surely people who felt as intensely as this about each other should not be apart? But they each had to go to their own home, each to their own family, each to their own room.

That had been the beginning of a glorious summer, the weekends of which were spent searching the moors; and in addition to the fascinating botanical specimens, they found many quiet places for their explorations and new-found interests. For the first time in her life, Annette found herself spending long hours alone with only one person... and that person was Brian.

The autumn was warm and dry and was equally welcoming, but in a different kind of way. Their outdoor activities had not been curtailed. The air was cooler, and the vegetation was changing, but she and Brian still had their time together outside on the moors.

Then November had come, with its news of Brian's move. His brother was to be married and was moving away to a house outside Birmingham that he had bought with Pat, who was to be his wife.

Annette and Brian had stared at each other miserably; and then, with the apparent resilience of the young, filled their winter with friends, visits to the museum, the cinema, and sometimes interesting talks. They planned how they would keep in touch by letter until Brian returned, although they had no idea when that would be. Once he was back, they would pick up their life where they had left off. They were sure about this.

But their plans had not worked out. Their contact by letter simply hadn't been what they had imagined. At first Brian's letters had been full of news. Hers had been her interested response, together with a description of her own doings and those of the friends they shared. But it became more and more clear that Brian had quickly plunged himself enthusiastically into his new environment, and found his new life was so satisfying that in his conscious mind she was quickly converted to a distant friend to whom he wrote about it all.

The intensity of Annette's feelings towards Brian began to shrivel, and she wrote less and less in response to his increasingly hurried and superficial letters. After all, she now had her own life at college to enjoy; and although unlike Brian she had no exciting change of country or continent, there was much to stimulate her young mind. The course was challenging, and some of her fellow students proved to be bright and stimulating companions.

As time went on there were plenty of young men who took an interest in her; and she began to enjoy social outings with a fellow student, Pierre, who was on an exchange year from Marseilles. They would go out with friends, and sometimes they would spend an evening together, relaxing in the large room he rented in a shared flat, talking and listening to music. His gentle touch was welcome to her, and she found it easy to respond.

When he left at the end of the year, she kissed him goodbye without feelings of loss. They exchanged a card from time to time. It was not long before she learned that his new girl friend was pregnant, and they were trying to find somewhere to live together. She wrote to wish them luck, but didn't bother writing again. After all, it might only complicate his life at a time when he was already overloaded; and Annette felt no need to keep up any contact.

She continued to live with her parents, who were warm, friendly people. They always welcomed her friends into their home. Although she felt she could trust them with everything, she had never spoken to them at the time about her deeper feelings for Brian, and later it hadn't seemed necessary. In fact it never crossed her mind to mention it to them. If she thought about it at all, she realised she had assumed that they must have guessed something of what had happened between them. They were intelligent, observant and sensitive, so it must have impacted on them in some way. She trusted them to have left it up to her to raise it if she had needed to, but she never had. After all she had felt as completely secure about Brian as she had about them. And when it finished...? Well... she had still believed for a while that he was there, even when he had gone away. By the time she realised he had gone forever, there did not seem anything to say.

There were times when she wondered if any of it had ever existed. She had certainly known him, because there were others who had been involved in their friendship, and they had frequented each others' homes. But those things they had done together on the moors...? They had only spoken to each other about that; and when he was no longer in real contact with her, it threw into doubt for her what had actually happened. Had it all been her fantasy? Some of it had, she knew, but not all of it... No, not all of it.

Her years of formal study completed, she got her first job – teaching at a large secondary school about five miles from her parents' home. Characteristically she threw herself into this new environment, soon offering activities after school, and becoming popular with the pupils because of her enthusiasm, availability, and obvious sense of equality in relating to them.

Annette had been a very late baby. Her mother was forty-five when she was born. Her parents had told her that they had always hoped to have children of their own, but as years went on they had faced the fact that this was very unlikely. They had eventually applied to the local authority social work department; and once screened, trained and registered, had for many years provided short term fostering for children whose parents were ill at home or in hospital.

Annette had always loved her parents' stories of the children they had cared for in their home during those years. They had so many happy memories of those times that they shared freely with her. As a child, she often remembered people in the street coming up to her mother and father showing obvious delight; and her parents would introduce her to yet another of their former charges, now grown up. It was an interesting situation, she reflected. It was as if she had a very large number of people in the community who were related to her in some way. And of course they were, although they were not blood relatives. Her relationship with them was a less usual, but quite special one. Her parents had loved and

7

cared for them all.

Her mind went back to her teaching post, and then to Tony. Tony was one of the chemistry teachers at school. They struck up a friendship in the first year she was there, but never met outside school hours. When she thought about their friendship, she realised that he was always a little distant in some ways; but this had never concerned her, as she had accepted it as part of his personality.

One day, during a chance conversation with another member of staff, she learned that he had been married, but that his wife had left him about a year previously. No one knew why, as Tony never spoke about her, and Annette hadn't felt it was appropriate to ask him anything about her.

During the summer term, she had asked him what he was planning to do over the long break, and was surprised to hear that he was joining an archeological dig in Denmark for six weeks. She was fascinated and intrigued, and this showed immediately in her questions. She found out how to make contact with similar projects, and learned that even at this late stage, it was sometimes possible to secure a place. Straight away she made applications, and was delighted when she learned she had been accepted as part of a team that was working on Shetland for four weeks that summer.

When she met Tony again at the start of the autumn term they had much to discuss; and by Christmas it had seemed quite natural to start researching the possibility of joining a dig together the following summer. They later secured places in a remote location in the Scottish Highlands, and spent many happy hours planning the trip.

That summer was idyllic. They travelled to the dig together in Tony's car, sharing the driving. The weather was perfect. The rest of the team were good to be around. Not only were they dedicated to the task, but also they were from a wide range of interesting backgrounds.

The site was surrounded by miles of heather – knee deep. Heather... Annette had felt a lurch inside when for a moment she remembered that other summer she had spent in the heather; but she quickly pushed the memory to one side, and immersed herself in the reality of *this* summer with Tony and her new friends.

During the last week of the dig, Tony had, uncharacteristically, suggested they went for a walk together in the evening. It had seemed natural to agree, and she had not thought to question the intention in his invitation. Maybe at the time he made it he had none; but as they walked along he reached out his hand to join hers, and began to talk to her of his growing affection for her. She was surprised and delighted, and said so.

After a few miles of warm exchanges, they had lain in the heather together, and wrapped themselves around each other, losing all track of time.

Eventually, the fading light alerted them to the fact that they should return to the others, who were polite enough to keep their guesses to themselves.

They did not attempt to repeat that evening; instead they concentrated once more on the task they had come to achieve. The long drive back was full of contented silences, interspersed with conversations about the dig, about school, and about possible plans of things they could next enjoy together.

When the Christmas break came, Tony set off to visit his parents in Hampshire for a few days, while Annette relaxed with her own parents, and two friends who could not get home for the festivities. The time passed pleasantly, and Annette looked forward to seeing Tony again when term began.

But something entirely unexpected happened. Two days before the beginning of term, Tony phoned her and asked her to meet him. He sounded excited, and somehow different from how she had known him before. Having exchanged a few pleasantries, they arranged, at his request, to meet for a local walk. The following day she set off in plenty of time to walk down to the car park at the start of the path. Leaning against the display board that bore details of the route and the wildlife, she wondered idly what she had picked up in Tony's manner on the phone.

He arrived a few minutes late, but that did not bother her. Drawing his car to a halt, he opened the door and got out eagerly to greet her.

'Annette,' he said, hugging her. 'You'll never guess what's happened!'

'What is it, Tony?' she asked, smiling at his excitement.

'Mary got in touch with me while I was at Mum and Dad's, and she came over to see me... We're getting back together again!'

Annette was stunned. She thought quickly. Tony had never mentioned his wife's name to her before. In fact she was sure he hadn't mentioned her at all, let alone her name. Yet somehow he expected her to know who Mary was. She presumed this must be his wife. But what could she say?

Struggling with her feelings, she asked, 'How did it all come about?'

He rushed on, oblivious of any impact his news might be having on Annette; or perhaps, in his almost child-like excitement, believing that the only feelings she could have were of pleasure and delight for him, as if she had been an older sister, or even his mother.

'She phoned out of the blue to see if I was there for Christmas, and asked if she could come over. She was staying with some friends about an hour's drive away. I said why didn't she come over that evening. She did, and we went and found a quiet place to talk. She told me she had always loved me, and that she knew she had made a terrible mistake when she left. She's coming back next month!' he finished excitedly, his face slightly flushed.

Annette observed his excitement, and found she could smile in a kindly way. It was obvious that he was completely wrapped up in his reaction to this turn of events, and had little or no grasp of who she was and how she might be feeling. He obviously regarded her as a friendly presence, but nothing more. Rapidly she detached her feelings and hopes from any thought of close relationship with him, and looked at her watch.

'That's great news,' she said generously. 'By the way, I should have said when we spoke on the phone that I don't have all that much free time today. I've got just under an hour left now, so shall we stroll along the path for twenty minutes or so, and then double back so I don't end up being late?'

She was glad that the path was too narrow to walk abreast. She found herself staring vacantly at the remains of the long dead fronds of bracken, brown and crumbling, while she heard Tony chattering away about his plans. She made herself say the occasional 'Yes', and 'I see', but did not worry that she could not hear most of what he was saying.

Back at the car park, she shook hands with him briefly, saying, 'It's good to hear your news, Tony. See you again soon at school.'

On the way back home she began to wonder if that evening she had walked with Tony was only a figment of her imagination. No... it wasn't. But that long twining in the heather could have been.

With the start of term, there was much to be done; and once more she threw herself enthusiastically into her responsibilities and the extra-curricular activities she had initiated. As always, she gained deep satisfaction from seeing the pupils respond by expanding their awareness and knowledge of the world around them. She saw very little of Tony. She would smile at him in passing, and he would raise his hand in acknowledgement; but they no longer approached one another for the eager conversations they used to share.

Several years passed, during which Annette felt deeply fulfilled by her work, and with her friendships and her life based at home with her parents. Then one day, while idly skimming the employment section of a national newspaper, she saw a job advertised that interested her. She showed it to her parents, who were very enthusiastic about it, and immediately supportive of her plan to apply. The college involved was some miles distant, and working there would mean much more time spent travelling, but the job would be an exciting challenge, and a good career move. She phoned for an application pack.

Annette set to work to update her CV, and had her application in well ahead of the closing date. Her parents began to speak to her about the possibility that if all went well and she got the job, they might begin to consider advancing some ideas they had; and she learned that they were thinking about sheltered accommodation.

At first she was upset by this, but they pressed her to talk it through with them. If she got the job, and found she was settled in it, they would be more than happy to make the move they had in mind. This in turn would release some of their capital, and with that they wanted to help her to buy her own home. The new post carried with it a better salary, and she would be able to take out a mortgage, which in addition to her savings and money from her parents, she could use to buy a substantial flat, or perhaps a small house.

Her mother had a heart condition that had worsened in recent years. She had had rheumatic fever as a child, and it had left her with a weakened valve. In the future she might find the stairs a trial, especially as the bathroom was upstairs. Rather than trying to adapt the house, her parents were beginning to feel that they wanted to find a good sheltered housing scheme, so that they were in a building that was easy for her mother. In addition to this, they thought that as Annette was their only child, they did not want her to feel burdened by them in their ageing years.

Annette received a letter informing her that she was on the short list for the job, and it gave her a date and time for her interview. When the day came, she dressed carefully in a smart brown skirt and matching jacket with a formal white blouse underneath, and set off in plenty of time.

11

Although she had been anxious, she found to her surprise that she enjoyed the interview. During the quite rigorous questioning by the panel, she sometimes forgot that she was being assessed as she spoke of her interests and of her hopes and aspirations for the education of young people. The following week she received a formal offer of the job, and she wrote back immediately to accept.

Her parents began to research their proposed move, and collected together a large file of information about sheltered housing schemes within reach of the college where Annette would be based. The most promising possibility was one that was shortly to be built, since a number of the units were to be at ground floor level, and single-storeyed. The fact that each of these had two bedrooms, and the living area opened on to a communal garden, made the proposition very favourable. There was even a row of shops within walking distance. They put their names down, together with a deposit.

By this time Annette had started her new job, and as before, had no difficulty in making more new friends.

It was not long after this that a curious turn of events arose. It was during the Christmas break, and Annette had been invited to the home of one of her new colleagues, Mike, where he was having a gathering. She arrived at the large post-war semi-detached house, to find the party in full swing. The door was opened by some friendly people, who introduced themselves as the next-door neighbours.

'Hi! We're Keith and Jane,' they said, holding the door open and welcoming her in. 'We're usually just through the wall, but we agreed to come round with some food and join in!'

Keith went on, 'Yes, and we've brought our friend too. He's staying with us this week.'

He pointed into the living area, and Annette froze. Surely it couldn't be...? But yes, it was... Brian! He looked a bit older of course, but certainly it was he.

'Is something the matter?' Jane asked, noticing the change in her demeanour.

'Oh... no... er... Actually, I've just remembered I forgot to send a text about a meeting I was trying to fix. I feel a bit silly. Would you mind if I stay in the hallway for a moment. It shouldn't take long.'

'Of course,' they replied; and they left her standing alone in the hall.

It was clear to her that Brian had not yet seen her. She wondered about leaving, but did not want to. She wanted to be at this party.

She took out her mobile, and addressed it in low tones. 'Okay, mobile,' she said. 'This is not going to be easy, but let's get on with it.' Then she put it back in her bag, and went into the room.

A girl with fair hair, who she guessed must be about thirteen or fourteen but looked as if she could be older, approached her with a tray of drinks. She thanked her, and took one that looked like lemonade. However, on tasting it she realised it must have something else in it too, although she was not sure what. She sipped it judiciously, and was joined by her host.

'Hello, Annette. So glad you could make it,' said Mike, patting her upper arm with a welcoming gesture.

'Hello, Mike,' she replied cheerfully. 'I see that you're in full swing already. Is that your daughter with the drinks tray?'

'Yes, that's Carrie,' he replied proudly.

'This drink has an interesting flavour,' Annette remarked.

'Ah, I expect you've picked one of my own concoctions. I've been experimenting with some spices, but I'm keeping the recipes to myself at the moment,' said Mike, with a deliberate air of mystery.

'It's always nice to try something new,' said Annette. 'Let me know if you ever decide to release the recipes to the general public!'

She felt steadied by this interaction, and decided to behave as if she had not noticed Brian, and to wait and see what happened. After all, she had come here to enjoy herself with her friends, and to meet new people. There was no reason to let his presence get in the way of that. But as she felt calmer, she realised that she was also curious about what had brought him here, and indeed what had happened to him since they were last in touch.

Her host went on. 'Can I introduce you to some old colleagues of mine from my last job?' he asked. 'They're biologists too, and I'm sure you'll have plenty to talk about.'

To her relief, he led the way across to the opposite end of the through-room, and introduced her to a pleasant couple who were sitting by the window. The hi-fi system poured a selection of relaxing music into the room, music which could only enhance conversation, and not impede it.

'Steve and Susan, can I introduce you to a new colleague of mine, Annette? She's in the same line of business as you.' He turned back to Annette and said, 'I'll leave you in the capable hands of my old friends. Do make yourself at home.'

She sat down on a vacant chair next to the couple, and Mike returned to the front of the house to look out for other guests who were still to arrive.

She was soon immersed in a fascinating dialogue with this older couple who had a lifetime of teaching behind them, and were only too keen to share their experience with her, and to listen with interest to hers. So involved did she become in this conversation that she completely forgot about Brian until she felt a tap on her shoulder. She turned round to see him standing there looking down at her.

'Excuse me,' he said politely to her companions. 'I don't intend to interrupt your conversation, but I would like to make my presence known to Annette. We knew each other some years ago.'

Annette rallied her inner resources and exclaimed, 'Brian! Goodness, what a surprise! The last I knew of you, you were in Dubai. What brings you here?'

'Actually, I'm a guest of the people who live next door. I'm here for the week. But don't let me butt into your discussion. Maybe we can catch up a bit later on in the evening.'

'Yes,' Annette replied. 'We could have a word later. There are a number of people I'm hoping to see this evening, but I'm sure there'll be time.'

Brian turned away, and she returned to her conversation, allowing herself to push him to the back of her mind. She knew she would have to think about him again shortly, but for now she wanted to engage with the others.

At length she rounded off her discussion with Susan and Steve. They insisted on giving her a note of their address and phone number in case she was ever passing their way, or wanted any information or resources they could provide. Carefully stowing the slip of paper in her handbag, she thanked them, and went off in search of others she intended to see this evening, and to find something to eat.

The time slipped by. The buffet that was spread round the kitchen was splendid; and she reflected on the time it must have taken to prepare it. There had been no indication that she should have brought something. Perhaps the neighbours' contribution had been substantial, or maybe Carrie was interested in cooking? In any case, it was wonderful.

What a pleasant evening this has been, she thought, looking at her watch. And now I must find Brian and have a few words with him before I leave. She noticed that there were fewer people now, and it was easy for her to spot him across the room. Their host had just handed a richly illustrated book to him, and he had begun to study it. She went across and addressed Mike.

'Thank you, Mike, for a wonderful evening.'

'I'm so glad you've enjoyed yourself, my dear,' Mike replied as he took her hand.

'There's one other person I must have a word with before I leave,' she said, nodding towards Brian. 'I don't expect you'll know, but Brian is someone I knew many years ago. It was a complete surprise to us both to see each other here, and we had arranged to speak before we left.'

'Of course. I'll get on with saying goodbye to others. Just take your time.'

He moved across to a couple who had appeared in the hallway in their coats, leaving Brian and Annette staring at each other.

'Where do you live now?' asked Brian simply.

'I'm with my parents at the moment,' she replied.

'Can I phone you tomorrow?'

Annette hesitated. 'Okay,' she said; and thinking it was safer to assume he no longer remembered her phone number, she began to open her bag for a pen, and asked him for something to write on. She knew instinctively that she was not willing to give him her mobile number.

He fumbled in his pocket, and then stopped. 'I think I can remember the number,' he said. 'It's just come into my head.'

He reeled off her number, and she nodded.

'I must go now,' she said, and left.

The next morning at breakfast she said to her parents, 'You'll never guess who I met at the party last night!'

Her mother looked across at her and said, 'No, I won't even try. Go on... tell me.'

'Brian,' said Annette.

'You mean Brian Wright?' her father asked.

'Yes,' replied Annette.

'Fancy that,' said her mother. 'What's he doing here now, and what's he been up to over the last years?'

'I don't know yet,' replied Annette. 'There wasn't really time to find any of that out last night. All I know is that he's staying with Mike's next-door neighbours for a week, and he's going to ring here today so we can fix to meet up.'

'Why not invite him round here, dear,' her mother encouraged. 'It would be good to see him. He used to come a lot at one time, didn't he?'

About midday the phone rang. Annette picked it up and heard Brian's familiar voice.

'Hello. Could I speak to Annette?'

'Speaking. Is that you, Brian?'

'Yes, of course. How are you this morning?'

'Fine, thanks. I enjoyed the party.'

'So did I. Mike's a good guy. I was glad to have the chance of meeting him. The party went really well. I didn't have a chance to speak to his daughter, Carrie, but she seemed very confident and relaxed for someone of her age. The friends I'm staying with explained about her mother. What a disaster for them!'

'Yes, it was a terrible thing to happen. She was killed in that road accident just before I started my new job, so I never met her.'

'Shall we fix a time to meet, and we can continue our conversation then?'

'Yes, of course. I was telling Mum and Dad about seeing you last night, and they're keen to say hello. When can you come down? I don't know how you're fixed today, but any time after three would suit us. Failing that, tomorrow evening would be okay.'

'Tomorrow evening would be fine. What time shall I aim for?'

'About eight.'

'I'll look forward to seeing you all then. Bye for now.'

And that was the start of it. When Brian came round they spent the evening catching up on some of the events of the intervening years; and they learned that he was getting ready to move back to his old haunts. In fact he had found somewhere to rent not far away, and was moving in quite soon. He had obtained a job at one of the local banks, but was hoping to develop his own business, providing IT support to small firms. He had made links already with the local Chamber of Commerce, and was discussing his plans with a small business advisor.

Before he left, he had made it clear that he was hoping to be in touch again very soon. 'We can do some more catching up,' he had said, as Annette let him out through the front door.

16

It was not long before Brian and Annette were spending time together every weekend. Although almost ten years had passed since they were last in touch, they seemed to fall back into an easy style of communication that belied their long separation. During the week Brian worked hard at the bank and on preparing to get his business venture off the ground, while Annette continued her work at the college, unstinting about the effort she put into it.

Her colleagues noticed a change in her. Although before she had been energetic in her application, now she seemed to be able to give even more; and she seemed to flow. 'Flow' was definitely the word that described her current state most accurately.

Her parents heard that there was a considerable delay about the completion of the sheltered housing scheme, but no one was worried about it. The wait of a further year or more did not concern them unduly. Annette would have more than ample time to search in a relaxed way for a place for herself. She and Brian felt in no rush to talk about living together. They were developing their careers while also enjoying spending regular time together, and that was sufficient.

Chapter Three

The day when Annette found her flat was exciting. But it was even more exciting when her offer for it was accepted, and at last she had her own home. That was the day for celebration! The timing had worked out very well. Her parents were due to move into their sheltered home about four months after she took possession of her flat.

Brian's business was beginning to take off, and soon he would leave his job at the bank. It was a risk, but it was one well worth taking. He had built up a network of promising links in the locality, and could hardly wait to get on with it all.

Weekends took on a different shape. Instead of taking time to go out together, Brian and Annette decorated her flat. She revelled in the task of choosing colours and fabrics, and Brian was only too pleased to help her with some of the DIY tasks she found it difficult to deal with on her own.

The day soon came when she could move in. There was still work to be done, but they had reached the stage at which she could live there while they were still working on it. The college holidays were not far away, and she looked forward to having plenty of time to work out exactly what she wanted for her home.

Once she was installed in her flat, her parents began to sort through their remaining possessions. They had, of course, given her pieces of furniture and household items she needed; but once that was done, they still had to work out what else to give away, as their new home was considerably smaller.

Annette loved her flat, and she loved the fact that Brian had been a part of her making it into her home. She loved to see the familiar things from her parents' house. She was grateful for their financial input, and she was proud of the fact that her own savings had been central to this venture.

And now, thoughts came into Annette's mind that she had not considered before. She had always got on well with young people, but she had never before thought of having children of her own. Now that she was installed in her flat she found she began to think of small children – and then she began to think of babies. She found herself fantasising about what it would be like to be pregnant... She found herself fantasising about *becoming* pregnant. Of course, it was Brian who featured in all her fantasies, and it seemed quite natural to her to want to start to share everything with him.

One Saturday evening as they lay on her bed together relaxing, she began to talk to him about what was in her mind. She said a little, and then waited for his reaction. She watched as a broad smile spread across his face, and he told her that he had been having these thoughts too.

'Go on,' he had encouraged. 'Tell me some more.' He had put his arms round her and held her tightly as they shared more of what they had been thinking, and they began to make tentative plans.

That night, they slept wrapped round each other. During the following weeks and months their resolve strengthened, and they began to tell her parents a little of their plans. They wanted to wait until Brian's work was properly established, and then they would think of living together.

But then everything began to change. Annette's mother became ill... very obviously ill. Her appointment at the cardiology department of the local hospital revealed that she now needed a replacement heart valve; and before her name came up on the list for the operation, she developed bronchitis that soon turned to pneumonia. She was taken into hospital, but never recovered.

Annette and her father were heartbroken; and despite all his attempts to keep his interests alive after the death of his wife, he simply wasted away. Annette used to spend her weekends with him, but he could not face going out. At first Brian used to go with Annette, but as the months passed he went less and less. Annette was so concerned about her father that she hardly noticed Brian's increasing absence, and just assumed that he was extra-busy at work. It was not until after her father's death the following year that she realised she was hardly seeing Brian at all.

Her commitment to her work remained unchanged. Throughout her life, she had never faltered in that: it was so important to her. Her parents had always supported and encouraged her in her studies and in her ideas and plans for her students, so that despite her grief for the loss of both of them she had no difficulty in continuing with her work. But she felt confused about Brian. She felt confused by his attitude, which she could only regard as being off-hand. Although he had known her parents well, he hardly mentioned them. Away from work she felt a great weariness, and she was unable to challenge Brian about his attitude.

As time went on, she rarely mentioned her parents to him. After all, there seemed little point; and she learned to reserve such conversation for her long-standing friends. The time Brian and she did spend together was full of awkward silences, and the little interaction they had was now usually only about work. There was no more talk of their future plans. None at all.

Then the day had come when he had made his announcement. Although the passage of years since then had meant it was no longer in the forefront of her thoughts, the memory of it was still etched on her mind. She had no difficulty retrieving it.

Brian hadn't invited her out for a while, so it came as a surprise when he suggested they had dinner at a small hotel in the countryside, which had a good reputation for interesting and unusual meals. She remembered feeling lighter after he spoke to her about it, and began to look forward to it. Saturday came, and she put on a dress that he had always liked – the one with the rather bold jungle colours on it. Then she chose her plain knitted grey jacket, and the bag and shoes that matched. Although it was almost dark when he rang the buzzer of her flat, the evening was warm and balmy, as it often can be in September.

As he drove he said nothing; but Annette felt quite relaxed, quietly confident that some change was about to take place in their relationship. In her bag, she had brought with her a tape of their favourite music; and suddenly remembering this, she took it out and inserted it into his tape player. The soft tones of the guitar duo filled the air. But did she detect a tension in him? Surely not.

She turned to him and asked, 'Shall I switch it off?'

'No. It's fine,' he replied; but she noticed his voice sounded unconvincing, and she began to feel a little anxious.

'Nearly there now,' he said, inconsequentially.

'Right.' Her response was almost mechanical.

Minutes later, he drew up outside a large converted farmhouse. There was a well-lit parking area there, with plenty of space.

'Come on then,' he said.

She took her bag and jacket, and got out of his ageing Cavalier. She did not wait for him. Instead, she slowly made her way up the steps to the front door where he caught up with her. He held the door open in a formal gesture which surprised her.

The receptionist smiled at them. 'Mr and Mrs Wright?' she asked.

Annette nodded as she noticed Brian faltering. A young man appeared, who showed them to a table in a quiet corner of the dining room. Although young, he was obviously well trained, she thought, as she observed the skill with which he manoeuvred her chair.

Brian remained silent, and she sat looking around. She noticed some interesting paintings hanging on the walls, and would have liked to examine them closely, but, strangely, she felt stuck to her seat. She had fairly long sight, but the lighting was very subdued, and she could not see as much as she wanted. She turned her attention to the other diners. She counted eleven tables, three of which were already occupied. One had places for ten people, all of which were filled. As she watched, it soon became apparent that there was some kind of celebration, and the people all appeared to be relaxed and jolly. She strained her hearing, but could not pick up enough to be able to detect what the celebration was about. The other two occupied tables were being used by older couples, who were possibly retired, judging by their appearance.

She turned to Brian, and said as cheerfully as she could, 'This is a very pleasant place.'

'Yes,' he replied.

She waited, and then tried again. 'Where did you find out about it? It's new to me.'

'Yes, I know,' he said in reply, and then paused.

Annette waited.

'I wanted to come to a place where we had never been before,' he continued. 'I asked around a bit, and then came up with this.'

He fell silent again, and Annette resumed her observations of the dining room.

After a little while the young man appeared with the menu, and bowing slightly, handed it to Annette who gratefully opened it for something to do. She looked through the choices, and realised that although she was hungry, eating was something she might find difficult. There was something odd happening, and she could not work out what it was.

She spoke to herself firmly in her thoughts. Now, it's no use not eating. Get something inside you, and then speak to Brian. Don't just sit there. Ask him what is preoccupying him.

'I'll start with salad,' she said decisively. 'How about you?' She handed the menu across.

'I'll have some lentil soup,' he said. 'What will you have after that?'

'Oh... the fish looks interesting,' she replied. 'I see they have a tarragon sauce with it.'

'I'm tempted myself,' mused Brian.

Annette was surprised at this, since she knew that at times when he felt distant from her, he invariably ate something different from anything she chose for herself.

He went on. 'But I think I'll have the beef.'

Annette absorbed this information, while the young man, who had seemed to reappear from nowhere, wrote their orders on a sheet of his small pad, and disappeared as mysteriously as he had come.

Beef, she thought. We haven't eaten beef at all over the last five years. We made a pact after reading that article about the way most beef is produced. She made no comment, but prepared to address him directly.

'Brian,' she said as she looked at him across the table. 'Brian. Is there something you want to talk to me about?'

He seemed to jump slightly.

'Er... no... I mean, yes. Yes, there is.' He waited for a moment as if gathering his thoughts, and then said, 'Annette, there's someone else in my life now, and I will be moving away from the area next month.'

Annette felt a torrent of feelings crashing inside her, but was incapable of putting any of them into words. Why had he brought her here to tell her? She stared at him, saying nothing. Her thoughts raced. How could he have been so duplicitous? How could he have told her in a place that was too public for her to allow any reaction?

'I think I could do with something to drink,' she said, in as dignified a way as she could muster. 'We should have ordered from the waiter. Would you mind going to the bar and getting me some sparkling water?'

His temporary absence gave her a few minutes to muster her thoughts. Never mind his reasons for bringing her here to tell her. He had told her, and that was it. It was obviously *un fait accompli*, so there was really no point in going into it all.

When he returned, she simply asked, 'Why didn't you say something to me before?'

His silence conveyed that he had no answer, so she did not pursue it.

The waiter came with her salad and Brian's soup, and they sat in silence while they ate.

Annette steadied herself by silently identifying the many leaves she found in her salad. Fortunately there were quite a number of different ones, and their names formed a mantra in her mind. Rocket, lollo rosso, iceberg, little gem... There was even some Italian parsley... good.

'Is your soup okay?' she asked, as lightly as she could.

'Fine.'

'Where are you going?'

He seemed to freeze, and then said, 'Abroad.'

'Oh,' she said. There didn't seem anything else to say. It was obvious that he did not want to let her know where he would be. What was the point of pressing him for information he was reluctant or unable to give?

'So you'll be away by the end of October?' she tried.

'Yes. That's right.'

The waiter removed her plate and his bowl, and soon returned with her fish, and Brian's beef.

I need this food, she said to herself, as she contemplated the task of eating it. She thanked the waiter, and picked up her knife and fork.

'I'm sorry, madam.' The waiter's voice penetrated her world. 'Could you wait a moment, please? I will bring you a fish knife.'

Annette felt tears spring into her eyes. His kind and courteous approach was too much to bear. Although she knew he only spoke like this because he had been trained to do so, the appropriateness of it was completely opposed to Brian's approach, and it allowed her pain to spill to the surface. Determinedly, she picked up her glass of sparkling water, and took a few small sips. It was obvious to her that Brian was in no condition to have a proper discussion with her, and she was no longer going to attempt to initiate one. Once she was back home she could take time to think about what she might do. Her task at the moment was to get this evening over as best she could.

As she worked her way slowly and carefully through her fish she searched for something to say, but found nothing. Brian too was silent as he chewed his beef mechanically, and almost belligerently. On the occasions when she glanced at him, she noticed that despite his chronological age he looked almost adolescent in his movements and gestures.

'That was very nice,' she announced as she mopped up the last of her tarragon sauce. Without giving him time to say anything, she went on. 'Brian. The food here is very good, but I don't think I need anything else this evening, and I think I would like an early night.' She looked at her watch. 'If we leave now, I should be back by ten. That would suit me very well.'

She noted something that she could only describe as unpleasant flash across Brian's face, and made a mental note that she could go home by taxi if necessary. This was not the time or place to ponder about this side of him – a side she had not seen before. The important thing now was to look after herself, and this meant going home.

Saying nothing, Brian went out of the room, and returned a few minutes later. She could see he was putting a credit card into his wallet. Before he reached the table, she put on her knitted jacket, picked up her bag, and began to walk towards the door.

'Annette...' he said, but stopped himself.

'Thank you,' Annette said to the receptionist at the desk.

Brian reached the car first. He unlocked the driver's door, got in, and released the passenger door. He drove her back to her flat in silence. He drew the car up and she got out. Before shutting the door behind her, she leaned down and said, 'I'll be in touch before you go, as there are one or two things we'll have to sort out.'

Then he was gone.

That night she took one of the sleeping pills the doctor had given her after her father died. She had preferred not to use them at the time, and they were still in the locked cabinet she kept in the bathroom. She wanted not to have to think for a few hours, and this medication might give her the break she needed. What she had just gone through had stretched her to her limits, and she needed a rest. Night-time was rarely a good time to think constructively. Tomorrow she would try again.

When she woke the next morning, she knew that something was wrong, but she could not at first work out what it was. She was in her bedroom... and in her bed. She was not ill... but she felt strange. She gazed at the pale green paint on the walls which she normally found quite calming, but now she found it surprisingly jarring. Why could that be? After all, it was the colour she chose for this room, and Brian had helped her put up the lining paper. Brian...!

It was then that the events of the evening came flooding back into her mind. She did not have to think any more. She knew straight away what to do. She lifted up the phone that was beside her bed, and keyed in a number that she knew by heart. She knew she needed to speak to someone she trusted about this, and the first person to try was Amy. Amy had been her friend since secondary school. Although she had not done biology, and had not been on the field trip where Annette had met Brian, she had been a close friend at the time. Amy had moved away to London when she took up her first job as a secretary; but they had kept in touch over the years, had visited each other, and had sometimes been away on holiday together. Amy had been so glad for her when Brian came back into her life. By that time she had met Joe, and they had married, and now had a daughter called Emma.

It was Emma who answered the phone. 'He...yo,' she said.

'Hello, Emma,' said Annette. The sound of Emma's voice brought a smile to her face. 'Is your Mummy there?'

She heard Emma put the phone down, and could hear her calling 'Mammy, Mammy. Lady, lady.'

Annette could hear brisk footsteps, and someone picked up the phone. 'Hello?' said Amy's voice.

'It's Annette here. Have you got some time to talk?'

'Oh, it's good to hear you. What a nice surprise! Yes, of course. Hang on a minute, I'll get Joe to play with Emma while we talk.'

Annette's voice wobbled a little as she told her friend about the change in Brian. Amy listened quietly, saying very little except to encourage Annette to keep talking.

When she had finished, Amy said, 'I have to be honest with you, I hate what Brian has done, and I feel very angry. My initial reaction is to phone him up and give him a piece of my mind! Or, better still, I'll tell Joe, and he can phone him.'

'Oh, no! Please don't do that,' begged Annette.

'I'm just giving you my reaction,' Amy reassured her. 'You know I wouldn't do anything unless you wanted me to.'

'Yes. I do know. It's just that I'm feeling pretty wobbly at the moment.'

'I'm not surprised,' said Amy reassuringly. 'Who wouldn't be, under the circumstances? I wonder what on earth's got into him. I've been waiting for you two to announce that you're moving in together, and now this instead!'

'Listen, Amy. Now I've told you what happened, can I ring off and phone you back later on? I need to take time to think. Are you in this evening?'

'Yes, I am. And do phone. Emma goes to bed about eight. We can have a long chat after that. And if you decide that you don't feel like talking after all, phone me anyway, just to say hello.'

'Thanks. Bye for now, then,' said Annette, and put the phone down.

After that she got up and wandered to the bathroom. The shower seemed a welcome prospect, and she let herself stand under it for a long time. The warm water caressed her body as it poured onto her shoulders and made its way by multiple routes down to her feet. Gratefully, she recalled the friendly plumber who had installed it for her. Plumbing had not been one of Brian's skills, and she could see that this was of great benefit to her now. She realised she felt secure in her shower cabinet. It was hers, and hers alone. She had chosen it, she had found the plumber; and when he came to install it, Brian had been busy at work, so he had never met him.

At length she felt strong enough to take the next step. She got out of the shower and reached for her towel off the heated rail. It was a towel her mother had given her when she moved here, and she clutched it round her, remembering her delight when her mother had produced it.

'It's not a very exciting present, love,' she had said. 'But I liked the sunflowers embroidered on the border, and I thought it would match the yellow in your bathroom.'

'Oh thanks, Mum,' she had replied enthusiastically, and she had given her mother a hug. Her mother... She had been a wonderful woman – warm, and loving, and sensible. She made her way back to her bedroom, wrapped in the memory of her mother's warmth, and sat on the edge of the bed.

I should get dressed now, she said to herself. She looked in the top drawers of her chest – a chest that had come from her father's family – and selected some matching underwear that was covered in tiny blue flowers. After that she put on her old jeans and a baggy overshirt. The shirt was not unattractive; in fact it was quite striking, being made from material in a batik style of bright blues and pale purple.

'Breakfast now,' she said aloud in firm tones.

'But I don't feel hungry...' she whispered.

'That doesn't matter,' said Firm Voice. 'You need something. Just have a piece of toast or some muesli, and eat it slowly. You'll be fine.'

She walked briskly to the kitchen; but there she was confronted by considerable difficulty. Brian had put a lot of work into this room. He had done most of the decorating; and because he had rewired the flat, he had

26

installed all the electrical points exactly as they had decided together.

Determinedly, she fixed her eyes on the blinds. These had been entirely her own choice. She had found a firm that produced some that were decorated with striking wildlife designs, and had surprised Brian by ordering them up secretly and fixing them herself. When he had come round the next evening, she had pulled them down with a flourish, and watched the amazement and admiration on his face.

She heard Firm Voice say, 'Blinds. My blinds.'

Although it was daytime, she pulled them down to fill the kitchen with the full effect.

Having done that she reached for the muesli. It was a kind that *she* liked, and Brian didn't. There was the end of a packet of the kind Brian preferred. For a moment she faltered; then she ran one blind up half way, opened the window, and poured the remaining contents of that pack into the bird feeder that was fixed to the other window with a suction pad. She felt strengthened by this action, and to her surprise enjoyed the small dish of muesli she had put out for herself.

'Dustbin liners,' Firm Voice directed, and she went to one of the drawers and took out the roll of black bin sacks.

'I can't,' said Whisper.

'You must,' replied Firm Voice, in tones that allowed no argument.

She tore the first bag off along its perforation and opened it out; then she returned to her bedroom and began filling it with the clothes Brian kept here.

'Pyjamas first,' said Firm Voice.

'Okay,' Whisper agreed.

After that there was no struggle. She did not feel good about it. Who would? But she felt confident of the rightness of her actions as she filled several bags with clothing, followed by a large cardboard box with CDs, DVDs, videos and books.

She lay down on her bed. Yes, *her* bed. Her father had bought it for her when she moved in. At the time, she had preferred to view it as a gift to both herself and Brian, but now she was happy to believe her father's original intention – that it was a gift to her alone.

Lying there, gazing at the special chest of drawers, she made her plans. It was so clear that there was no point in arguing or remonstrating with Brian. His mind was obviously made up, and must have been fixed for a while. She had no idea how long ago he had made his decision. She knew now that because she had been so preoccupied with the illness and loss of her parents, she had not noticed the change he had been undergoing until it was too late. He was closed to her; and there was no point in wasting her breath.

She thought how she would have to find some way of getting his possessions to him. She knew that she did not want to do it herself. She would see him one more time, but not to hand over his things. She pondered the possibilities. It did not seem right to involve someone they knew to help with the possessions, so she would have to think carefully. She turned her mind to how she might arrange a final meeting, but now her clear thinking scrambled.

Firm Voice took over once more. 'Go for a walk,' it said. 'Now! And *don't* go out on the moors.'

Obediently, she put on a pair of strong shoes and her lightweight anorak. Soon she was walking along the road that led to a series of field paths that provided a circular route. As she watched the cattle in the fields, she reflected upon the relative simplicity of their lives. They watched her with what appeared to be mild and passing curiosity as she made her way alongside them and eventually out of sight.

As her circulation stirred with her brisk strides, she could see straight away what to do with Brian's possessions. It was simple. She would contact a local taxi firm to see if they would take on the job of transporting them. Then she could write him a note saying that his things would be delivered on a particular evening. Even Whisper felt confident that she could find someone, so she turned her mind to the problem of a final meeting.

This was more tricky, she thought. Certainly, it should not be at his place or at her flat. As she considered possible venues, she realised that she did not want to see him in a building: it had to be outside. Outside... but where? Then she knew the answer to her question: The Garden of Remembrance.

After her mother's cremation, she and her father had scattered the ashes together there, in a private and purely personal ceremony of their own. She had never spoken to Brian of this. She wondered now if her decision to keep this to herself had arisen from some faint sense that her relationship with him was not quite right. She dismissed this idea, and thought on. After her father's cremation, she had gone back to the Garden one day and had quietly scattered his ashes in the same place. Again, she had never said anything about this to Brian. Once more she wondered if her failure to tell him had arisen from something she had sensed about their relationship. But there seemed no point in pondering about that now.

How could she get Brian to agree to her chosen venue? she asked herself. Then she realised there would be little difficulty if she suggested they met in the park next to the Garden and the graveyard that continued on from it. He would not think the park to be a strange place to meet. It had represented an ordinary, unremarkable feature of their lives. Yes, they could meet there, and then she could go through the gate into the Garden of Remembrance as she left him. She could be there afterwards... without him, but not alone. That was a better idea.

Confident about what she had decided, she completed her walk and returned to her flat. Wishing to advance her plan about his possessions, she opened the Yellow Pages to look for details of local taxi firms. Her third attempt put her in touch with a pleasant young man, who, keen to expand his business, was more than willing to undertake this slightly unusual task.

'Yes, that's right,' she said to him. 'I have a friend who's going abroad soon. He's in rented accommodation at the moment, and had stored some of his things at my flat. It would be very helpful if I could pay you to take them across. We're both rather busy at the moment, and it will save us time.'

This arranged, she took out her writing paper and penned a note to Brian:

> *Brian,*
> *Mr Hood, of Able Taxis, will deliver your possessions at 8p.m. on Wednesday evening. I will pay him before he leaves here.*
> *Can we meet for a short time by the wrought iron seat in the park? I suggest Saturday at 1p.m.*
>
> *Annette*

Having gone over what she had written, she put the note in an envelope, added a first class stamp, and ran down the stairs and along the street to the post box at the T-junction. Good, she had just caught the Sunday collection.

Well done, she thought as she retraced her steps up to her flat. She put the bags and the box in the cupboard off the hallway to be out of sight, and sat down in an armchair in the sitting room – the chair where she usually sat. She suddenly felt very weary. She allowed herself a little time, and then began to organise her thoughts.

There seemed to be three immediate issues. She must keep eating – and she was aware that lunch was long overdue. She had work to finish preparing for tomorrow. She must do something with the chair that was staring at her from the other side of the room and making her feel very uncomfortable – the chair that Brian had habitually used.

Having decided that the first priority was food, she went to the kitchen and examined the store of cans of soup she kept there for emergencies. Lentil... that sounded good. Oh... no. Perhaps not for a while. She looked at the next can. Winter vegetable, she read. Yes, that would be fine. She opened it, poured the contents into a small pan, and put it on one of the halogen rings of her cooker. She looked in the fridge and found the end of a loaf of soda bread, which she spread with vegetable margarine.

She sat at the small kitchen table, and was surprised to find that eating was not as daunting as she had thought it might be. As she ate, more slowly and carefully than usual, she let her mind work its way round the problem of the chair. It was the twin of the chair that she herself used. The pair had been donated by friends who had been moving house, and were buying new furniture. She regarded the chairs as belonging to her flat, and saw no need to go through the motions of offering one to Brian. After all, it was almost certain that he would not want it, and she would have to cope with more bad feeling after mentioning it, and being further rebuffed.

Then she had an inspiration. Leaving her food half eaten, she went to the cupboard in the spare bedroom, and pulled out the throw that Amy had once given her some years ago. She had always liked it; but having no immediate use for it, she had stored it away. As she pulled it out and spread it on the spare bed, she once more admired the deep purple colour, decorated with a design worked in gold threads. She went back to the cupboard and rummaged in her sewing box for two large blanket pins. Then, gathering up the throw together with the pins, she walked purposefully to the sitting room. She arranged it over the chair that Brian would no longer be using, and pinned it in place.

Stepping back a few paces, she admired her handiwork. What better reason for using it? And it looked very good. She made a mental note to be sure to tell Amy that evening when she phoned her.

Remembering her bread, she returned to the kitchen, finished the rest of it, tidied up, and went to get her document case. She would use the table here, finishing her preparation for work for the coming week. Deliberately, she put her chair so that whenever she looked up she saw the window. She raised the blinds half way. There was an agitated flutter of feathers, and she realised she had disturbed a bird that had been pecking muesli from the feeder.

'Sorry,' she said. She hoped it would return.

She had no difficulty in concentrating on her work. It was fortunate, particularly in her state of extreme stress, that all her associations with it were good.

Apart from their having first met on that field course, Brian's work and hers had been quite different. Each took an interest in what the other was doing, but there was no overlap. They had enjoyed many things together, but work was not central. She thought again of her numerous friends and colleagues who worked in the same field as herself, and felt supported. She thought again of the great interest her parents had taken in her studies and her work, and a special warmth crept through her.

She put her papers carefully back into her document case, and remembering that eating was something that she may have to pay special attention to for quite some time, she decided to devise some strategies to help herself. Saturday evening was likely to be the worst time, since Brian and she had made a habit of spending that evening together, sometimes alone, and sometimes with mutual friends. Apart from that, Wednesday evening was the time they were the most likely to meet.

She made a short list of people that she would tell soon about Brian's impending departure, and then she began to think of friends who might share meals with her at weekends.

By the time she phoned Amy that evening, not only had she made her lists, but also she had cooked a large pan of thick soup, some of which she ate, and the rest she froze in portions for the week ahead. She was grateful to have a long conversation with her friend, telling her about everything she had done that day. Amy was clearly outraged about Brian's behaviour, but hadn't pressed her views on Annette. The only thing she insisted on was that she phoned Annette later in the week; and she also encouraged her to phone any time she wanted.

Mr Hood arrived promptly at a quarter past seven on Wednesday; and by half past, the bags and box were gone. Annette had been grateful for the sound of his whistling, and for his cheerful manner. He had filled her flat with something new, if only for a few minutes, while helping her to remove the remains of the old.

When she came in from work on Thursday, she found the post included a letter from Brian. She opened the envelope straight away, and found a slip of paper inside which merely stated:

Saturday is okay. See you at the seat.

Brian

She tore it into small pieces, put it in the kitchen bin, and buried it amongst the potato peelings and outer leaves of the sprouts she had eaten the day before.

Saturday came, and she prepared herself carefully. The day was quite cold, and she put on the grey woollen dress she had worn at her mother's funeral. Under her full-length grey winter coat, this would be entirely hidden from view, which was what she preferred. She selected a small book of poems that had been a favourite of her mother's, and put it in her handbag.

She left her flat at mid-day so that she could walk in the grounds of the crematorium for a while before she was due to meet Brian. She valued the time she spent reading inscriptions on some of the gravestones in the adjoining graveyard before making her way to the Garden of Remembrance. Once there, she stood for a while before continuing through the gate and into the park.

She reached the seat with five minutes to spare, and sat and waited. One o'clock came, but there was no sign of Brian. She reached into her bag and took out the book of poems. She opened it at random, and fixed on a verse she found there. She noticed that it was entitled *Kindness*, and it reminded her of everything she had ever received from her parents.

She read through it silently, and then spoke it out in low murmuring tones. Greatly calmed by its message she turned to others; but she later returned to that original verse and read it out again, this time more audibly.

So immersed was she in her book, she had not noticed anyone approaching, and she jumped as she heard a voice say, 'That's one of my favourites too.'

She looked up and saw an older woman smiling at her.

'You startled me,' she said.

'Yes, I know,' replied the woman. 'I didn't mean to. I'm sorry. Can I see the cover of your book?'

'Certainly,' said Annette, holding it up.

'Ah, I wondered,' said the woman. 'I thought that might be the one. It's the same as the one my husband bought for me on our first wedding anniversary. It's very special to me.' She paused, and then went on, 'He's not with us now.'

'I'm sorry to hear that,' said Annette, in genuine tones. 'I'm glad you have this book too. This copy was my mother's.' She glanced at her watch. 'Goodness!' she exclaimed. 'It's half past already. I was waiting here for someone, but I think he's not coming after all.'

'What a shame,' replied the woman. 'I expect there's an explanation.'

'Yes, I expect so too,' replied Annette. 'I must go now, but I'm very pleased to have met you,' she said sincerely.

'I want to tell you it's meant a lot to me seeing you with that book today, and hearing you reading from it,' said the woman. 'It would have been my husband's eightieth birthday today.' She reached out her hand and touched Annette's arm briefly. Then she turned, and was gone.

Annette put the book in her bag, and made her way back to the Garden of Remembrance. She did not expect to hear from Brian again. Standing by the area where her parents' ashes were scattered, she took her mother's book out of her bag once more, and read several poems from it.

After that, she walked home to continue the life without Brian that she had already begun. Although she had regular conversations with Amy, and she told all the people she needed to that Brian was moving away, she rarely mentioned him after that.

Chapter Four

Annette sat in her chair with tears coursing down her cheeks. She made no attempt to stop them, or to move from her chair.

At length, she slowly became aware that the light was beginning to fade, but she did not switch on a lamp. Such action was not necessary: she needed no artificial illumination. On an overcast November afternoon, it might only be four o'clock, she guessed. She did not look at her watch. She was enveloped in a great exhaustion – an exhaustion which totally consumed her, and allowed no energy for irrelevances.

Somewhere inside she was sure that what she was doing now was right for her; and although it felt terrible to be in this state, she knew it was somehow necessary. After all, she had made the decision to spend time today trying to search for clues to the elusive state that was bothering her. Well, she thought, it hadn't taken long, had it? And when it had begun to show itself, so much had rushed into her consciousness that she had needed to be completely still in order to withstand the intensity of it.

Time passed; and although no more memories had come into her mind in the last while, she knew she was right to stay where she was. She was still, apart from the movement of tears down her cheeks, her intermittent use of tissues to absorb them, and the rise and fall of her chest with her now less frequent sobs.

The room had darkened considerably, and Annette began to realise that she was feeling cold... very cold. In fact, she felt something more than coldness. She felt deeply shocked. When she got up to go into the hall to switch on the central heating she stumbled, and realised that her feet were almost numb with cold.

Then she went into her bedroom and got a pair of thick socks, which she put on before pushing her feet into her roomy slippers. Her tears had stopped now, but she returned to her chair, wanting to feel the security of it around her while she took stock of her situation. Here she was, forty-three years old. She had a satisfying job, a nice flat, and plenty of friends and colleagues. But for a while she had known there was something wrong, something she had never quite been able to put her finger on. Taking time for herself today, she had got nearer than ever before to what that was. She knew it was certainly something to do with being upset. And it was something to do with all the memories that had flooded into her mind as she sat in her chair, crying.

She sensed there was more to come, and decided to stay quietly in her chair. She wanted to give it time. She realised vaguely that this might hasten its later emergence. Her head felt empty now, but not in an unpleasant way; and she realised that the elusive 'absence' she had felt before had been to do with something she had been holding back, rather than something that wasn't there. Her limbs felt heavy with a particular kind of relief, and she waited.

A thought came into her mind, unbidden. The photograph albums... She looked across at the framed photograph of her parents that she kept on the fire shelf. It was her favourite – a photograph of them with their first foster child. She had an irresistible impulse to go to her study and get the old albums she kept there in a drawer of her desk. Without stopping, she almost ran through the hall, took the albums out of the drawer, and returned to the safety and security of her chair. Slowly she turned back the soft red cover of the first one. It began with a photograph of her parents on their wedding day, standing outside her grandmother's cottage. Annette remembered her maternal grandmother a little, because she had not died until she was about seven.

She turned page after page, studying once again the photographs of her parents' first home, and of many of the children they had fostered. She derived great comfort from this activity, and wondered why she had not looked at these photographs for so long.

The first album finished, she turned to the second. It had a stiff dark green cover. She stroked it meditatively before opening it. This was the album that began with a photograph of her mother, who was very obviously pregnant. Annette smiled, and then studied the pictures of herself as an infant, cradled in her mother's arms. Her mother was radiant, and her eyes were lovingly joined with the gaze of her baby. Picture after picture showed scenes from Annette's childhood – her first day at the weekly nursery run by the local church, her first day at school, her birthday parties... She treasured each image and the memories attached to them, as she made her way slowly through the album.

She sighed. She felt warmed by what she had seen; and in a way she felt back at an earlier time of her life, perhaps about ten years old, living in a secure, loving home.

Her hand hovered over the last album with its dark navy cover. This, she well knew, started with her first day at secondary school. Well, there was no harm in looking at the one of herself in her new uniform. She had been very proud of it. The colours had suited her well – dark navy, with golden yellow braiding. She opened the cover, and studied the first page. She looked so eager on that day, and her eagerness about her studies had never faltered since then.

She hesitated again. If she looked through many more pages she would soon come to the photograph that Steph had taken of her and Brian on that field trip. And soon after that she would see the ones her parents took of Brian when he arrived on his new bike one weekend. And there were more of him after that. She felt herself grow tense. What should she do? If she looked at them, she must really feel what they meant to her then, and what they might mean to her now.

She wondered whether to phone Amy. It would be so nice to speak to her, she thought. Actually, it would be nice to speak to Emma too. She had started secondary school just over a year ago, and her enthusiasm about her studies reminded Annette of herself at that age. But she knew that pleasant though such conversations would be, they would be a distraction from what she needed to do at the moment. She knew instinctively that difficult though the path she had embarked on was, it was the most important thing at the moment.

She returned to her deliberations about the third album, and soon realised that she should not back off now. She took a deep breath, then she turned the pages and studied the next pictures. She was glad to find that she did not grow tense again as she looked at them. In fact, she noticed that there was a tinge of curiosity in her mind as she contemplated the images of Brian. As she turned page after page she found her reaction did not vary each time she saw him.

There were more pictures of him than she had remembered, intermingled with ones of countryside scenes and photographs of other friends. There were even a few of friends' pets. And here was Bounce, the mongrel puppy that came to live next door when she was about sixteen. She remembered how she used to take him for walks.

Her mind drifted back to that last meal she had shared with Brian, ten years ago. What exactly was it about him that had been so different and disturbing? Was there any indication of that part of his personality when she had first known him? She searched her mind, but could not identify anything. The one thing she was sure about was that stab of disquiet, almost fear, that she had had sitting across the table from him that evening. She went back through the album, scrutinising the photographs of his adolescent form, but came up with nothing.

She closed the album, and then sat quietly for a while, thinking. It had seemed such a huge step to take; yet, now she had done it, it did not seem very remarkable. Good, she thought. The feeling I had about the photographs was out of date with what they mean to me now. What a shame I did not look at them before, but perhaps I was not ready to. She got up and returned the albums to their drawer in the study.

She had other photographs of Brian that had been taken after they met again the day of Mike's party. These included a few of the time they spent together working on getting the flat ready for her.

'Maybe I'll make something nice to eat now,' she said aloud. 'And then I'll look for those other photos.'

She went into the kitchen and took a portion of soup from her freezer.

'Butternut squash – my favourite!' she exclaimed.

She switched on Classic FM, and a Strauss waltz filled the room.

Almost satisfied after the soup, she completed her meal with oat biscuits and peanut butter.

She did not know exactly where to look for the photographs, and began by searching some boxes from the cupboard in the hall. Turning to the built-in wardrobe in her bedroom, she soon discovered where they were. Spreading them out on the kitchen table, she saw that there were certainly many that included Brian. These were the pictures of the man who was to be her husband, and perhaps the father of her children. She felt sad, but not because Brian was not with her. And she knew that her sadness was to do with discovering that he was not the person she had believed him to be.

Then something struck her. It was so obvious that she wondered how she had not thought about it before. Since Brian went out of her life ten years ago, she had not been in a close and intimate relationship with any other man. How on earth could this have happened?

She sat down heavily on one of the kitchen chairs. There had been Brian. Then there had been Pierre, and then there had been Tony. After that, Brian had come back into her life, and as time went on they had planned their future together. When he went, all her intimate life had gone with him. How could this have come about? Its disappearance hadn't been the result of a conscious decision.

She thought about her wide circle of friends and colleagues. She was fond of them all, men and women, single or with partners, people of all ages. Why was it that she had not engaged in any closer relationship with anyone? It had not even occurred to her that she might. She found this extraordinary realisation very upsetting.

She knew now that she was getting nearer to the source of the nebulous feeling that had been troubling her; and disturbing though it was she was determined to persist. She stood up, and began to walk through the flat. She went out of the kitchen and into the hall, into her study, her bedroom, her spare room, her bathroom, the sitting room, and back along the hall to the kitchen. She discovered that there was something surprisingly grounding about that exercise, and she repeated it.

She could hear something... a buzzing sound... a bee, perhaps? But there couldn't be a bee, not in her flat, nor at this time of year. Yet, there it was... the buzzing. By this time she was out in the hall again. She stopped, stock-still. The buzzing continued; and it was then that she realised this sound was in her head. But why?

Then it struck her that she might be remembering something. But what was it?

She felt a warmth rush through her body. Puzzled, she looked down at her hands and arms, as if expecting them to tell her. She became aware of a prickly sensation on the backs of her legs, and she went to the mirror, and turned her back, trying to look over her shoulder to see. There was no sign of inflammation, yet the uncomfortable prickling sensation persisted.

She felt puzzled, and mildly frustrated. What did all this mean? But although she spent the rest of the evening alternately pacing and sitting thinking, she got no further forward.

As she got ready for bed, she comforted herself with the knowledge that she had achieved quite a lot today. She still had not got to the bottom of what was troubling her so much, but she had clues that might eventually lead her there.

She wriggled down under the duvet in her cosy pyjamas. She felt tired, and was glad to switch off the bedside light.

She woke suddenly in the night, and sat bolt upright, feeling intensely anxious. Was I dreaming? she wondered. But she had no memory of any dream. She switched on her swan light, and found herself examining her forearms. Almost immediately she noted that the prickling on the backs of her legs was still there.

'Oh, never mind!' she exclaimed in exasperation. She switched off the light and wriggled down under the warmth of the duvet once more. At least that bee had stopped buzzing.

The next morning she came to slowly. Bees, arms, prickling and heather all seemed to be muddled up in her mind. She tried rolling over and going to sleep again, but it didn't work. Her head felt slightly sore, as if it were too full of something.

Eventually she got up, and it was when she was having her shower that things began to fall into place. She left the water running, as this seemed to help. Running water... a small stream... heather... *the* heather... prickling... a bee. Yes, that all went together.

Now she could remember lying in the heather with Brian, in that very special place they had found together. Yes, there had been other quiet places where they had been close, and they had all been special; but this place had been the most special – the place where they had been at their most intimate. She shuddered momentarily, and this surprised her. Perhaps she was getting cold? The water was still warm.

She turned the water off, reached for the towel, and wrapped it round herself. As she dressed she began to wonder if there had been something that she had not been entirely happy about in that place – perhaps something that linked with the feeling she had had about Brian the last time she saw him? She found herself looking down at her arms again, not knowing why; and she wished that her father was there to speak to.

Her father had been so kind, quiet, and gentle. She knew she could approach him about anything. After his death she had never stopped missing him. For quite some time this had been with a more ordinary sadness, but now she fervently wished he was here. She longed to be able to speak to him; and although she had not got a clear idea of what she might say, she was sure that she would be able to talk about what was troubling her.

Annette felt very uncomfortable in the intensity of her feeling. It was so strong that it threatened to overwhelm her. She was tempted to try and divert her thoughts on to something else – *anything* else; but she knew that was the wrong thing to do. Slowly she put on her clothes, and gradually her thoughts led her to the Garden of Remembrance, and her mother's book of poetry. She had not been back there for a long time. She remembered again the day Brian failed to meet her in the park – the day that was to have been her final meeting with him – and she remembered the comfort she had derived from the Garden and her mother's book.

She hurriedly ate a piece of dry toast, put her book in her bag, put on her coat and shoes, and was soon hurrying down the road in the direction of the park. She wanted to enter the Garden from the park. After fifteen minutes of brisk walking she could see the gate. When she reached the wrought iron seat, she broke into a jog, and almost burst through the gate into the Garden, where she stopped, slightly out of breath.

She took the book from her bag. *The Golden Treasury of Modern Lyrics Volume II* was embossed on the spine in the familiar gold lettering. She opened the first page, and began to read:

Since to be loved endures,
To love is wise:
Earth hath no good but yours,
Brave, joyful eyes...

This was one of her mother's favourites – written by Robert Bridges. But at this moment she was not concerned about who had written it. The most important thing was that it had been special to her mother.

She turned the pages, and kept reading. At times she hardly knew what the words were trying to convey, but it did not matter... she read on.

After some time she felt calmer, and sat quietly on the wooden seat, with her book and her bag in her lap.

On her return home, she resolved to work out why she had forgotten about intimacy between a man and a woman, and to find a way forward. She knew now that her tears of yesterday had been for herself. Yes, she still missed her parents, and she knew she always would. No, she did not miss Brian. There had been something wrong in her relationship with him. Maybe she would never know properly what it was, but perhaps that did not really matter.

The greatest grief in her life now was the realisation that she had, somewhere along the way, lost a part of herself... and she had lost touch with it to the extent that she had forgotten its very existence.

'I am forty-three years old,' she said quietly, as she took off her coat.

'I have many years ahead of me, and it is very important that I lead a life that is truly mine. I am true to myself in my work, and in my friendships, but I have left something of myself behind somewhere, and I need to find it again.'

She searched her mind to decide to whom she could talk about this, but to her surprise could not come up with anyone. Out of the many people she knew and trusted, there was no one she felt she could approach. There must be a reason for this, she reflected. Perhaps it is something I must embark upon alone, for the moment at least? she asked herself.

It was later that evening, when she sat curled up in her armchair, which she had drawn close to the gas fire, that a plan began to form in her mind.

From time to time that evening she had dipped once more into her mother's poetry book, and she had not long finished reading *The House Beautiful* by Robert Louis Stevenson, when it came to her. She ran over his lines again:

> A naked house, a naked moor,
> A shivering pool before the door...

She could make a beautiful house for herself, and she could make a beautiful relationship – one that was entirely right for her. She could make it all in her imagination. She wanted to feel free and confident about her intimate relating, and this seemed entirely the right way to begin. She wanted to know herself in great detail, and to feel completely secure in this. This decision was her first step. And she would do whatever it would take, safe in the privacy of her own home, whenever she wished.

She closed the book and put it away, grateful that it had provided the final prompt.

She took instead a pad of paper and a pen, and began to write...

Chapter Five

17 May

May, yes May was a good month to begin. Everything would be bursting into leaf, and the air would be warming up, although the nights could still be cold.

She would write a letter to her lover – a 'paper lover'. He would only ever exist in her mind, and on her sheets of paper; but she needed him to be there, so that she could write to him and decide how she wanted to enjoy her life with him.

Now, she needed a name... She leaned back in her chair for a few minutes, while she debated what it would be. How about 'Peter'? Yes, Peter... that name would be all right. She didn't want to use any of the names of people she had been involved with before, or indeed the name of anyone she knew well. She wanted an ordinary kind of name, nothing pretentious. 'Peter' would do fine.

What next? She hesitated, put down her pad and pen, and went to the kitchen for a cold drink. She felt agitated. No, she didn't; it was more a state of alertness. She returned to her chair and picked up her pad and pen again. First she needed a context. What should it be? Heather? No, not heather, she said firmly to herself; and she smiled as she recognised the resonance of that Firm Voice of ten years ago that had been of such help to her in her hour of need. It needs a different context, she murmured to herself. Perhaps some trees...?

Then she began to write:

Dear Peter,

I certainly like a cold and windy afternoon, with the trees tossing. I would like to be outside with you in the wind, walking together through the trees. I love to see the movement of them. I can't describe how much that means to me. I want a bedroom where I can see the trees when we are lying on the bed.

She read through what she had written, and felt pleased with it. At the moment she did not need to know much about Peter. All she needed to know was that he was there in her mind, whenever she wanted. She stroked her pen gently for a moment, and then wrote more:

When you approach me to come closer, please always gently kiss the inner part of each wrist, both of my ankles, my neck, and also, fleetingly, my mouth and between my legs. I want to hear you say your name. Then we must hold each other for a while. After that we can begin.

Again, she read through what she had just written. She sighed. This might be exactly the right thing to do. In any case there was every reason to try it out. After all it was where her thoughts had led her.

She read through both the paragraphs. After that she closed her pad and took it to her bedroom. She opened the bottom drawer of the chest, and reached for her father's favourite scarf – the one her mother had given him on their honeymoon. Carefully, she placed the pad in the drawer, and put the scarf on top of it. Tomorrow she would be starting the week's work. Her pad would be safe here, and she could continue writing when the time was right. Now she needed to sleep.

She slept very deeply, and woke the next morning feeling relaxed and restored, just before the alarm went off. Her mind felt clear as she got ready for work, and she looked forward eagerly to the first class of the day.

The end of term was soon upon her. The Christmas break was to be quite busy. She was staying with Amy, Emma, and Joe for a week, and was then coming home to prepare her flat for a New Year party. After that was over, she intended to spend time getting ready for the following term.

She had not forgotten the pad at the bottom of the drawer in the chest, but she felt no need to return to it at the moment. It was enough to know that she had made a start, and she knew she would take it out again when the right time came. Somewhere in her mind her new correspondence was developing, and she could return to it later.

It was not until the following term had advanced by several weeks that she felt she wanted to return to her pad. She was spending a quiet Friday evening alone. Once more she was curled up in her chair in front of the gas fire, and she had put her pad and pen on a small table nearby.

Presently she began to chuckle as ideas came into her mind, and she picked up her pen.

5 July

Yes, July. Let's have July now... the summer. She wrote:

Dear Peter,

I do like the name Peter, she thought. I have known him for a few months now, and the name has become quite pleasant and familiar to me.

Thank you so much for your letter, it arrived yesterday morning. I opened it, but almost immediately decided to put it away until night-time, when I would be alone in bed. I wish you had been there to see the smile spread wider and wider across my face as I read it.

A scene came into her mind. Why not just write it down? she reasoned. There was certainly no harm in doing so. And she wrote:

That night I imagined being with you, Peter, and this is what happened: When you weren't looking, I crept noiselessly across the floor, and from the bedside table I stole your watch and your clock, and I hid them, deep in a drawer full of sweaters, where you would never find them. Time no longer existed. Important meetings? Tomorrow? Irrelevant! There was only one important meeting on this earth, and it was happening then. I signalled for you to be silent and to lie perfectly still. I joined you, and joined with you. We entered a state of being-ness, in which thoughts do not exist.

When I woke the next morning, it was with images of lying on you and gently nibbling at your left ear lobe, tonguing round inside your ear. I wanted you to sit up so I could be astride you, with you inside me. We stayed like that, kissing, until you couldn't hold back any longer. As some of our wet gradually leaked out of me, I collected it up in my fingers to smear on my face and lips.

On rereading what she had written, Annette was more than satisfied with the stealing of the alarm clock, and she laughed out loud. Briefly she recalled how, towards the end of her relationship with Brian, she had begun

44

to sense that he had fabricated the existence of some Saturday morning meetings, for which he claimed to need to leave her flat by seven thirty at the latest.

She wasn't too sure about the rather explicit sentences at the end. She was entirely unused to writing like that, and although it was a part of what had come into her mind, it felt odd seeing it on the page in front of her.

She reminded herself that her writing was for her and her alone. She was doing it purely for herself; and she had a right to put down whatever came into her mind. In a way it was a good thing to see it written on the paper. It helped her to think about it, and she could decide whether or not it was something from the person she truly was, or if it in any way included a resonance of things she had felt drawn into – things she had not been quite sure about.

She was tired, and felt she had written enough for now. She closed the pad and put it away in the drawer.

The next day, Saturday, was taken up with a trip to the local supermarket, followed by joining a group of friends that were visiting a small art gallery to see an exhibition by a local artist. Annette was tempted to buy a small scene of a local view of the river, and on impulse put her name on it and paid a deposit.

Afterwards the group ate out together, and Annette arrived back home quite late. Despite this she felt wide awake; and finding she was still hungry, she settled herself in front of the fire with a mug of hot soup. She sipped it meditatively, enjoying memories of the pleasant day she had spent with her friends.

The soup finished, she thought again of her pad at the bottom of the drawer, and went to fetch it. Settling herself once more in her chair in front of the fire, she noticed she felt something that she could only describe as 'daring'. She began to write once more.

10 July
Dear Peter,

Have you ever seen anchovies in oil in small narrow glass bottles? I sometimes think of these as sperm in a vagina. This is my secret way of remembering our lovemaking, while I am busy working in the kitchen. When I eat these things, it conjures up for me such strong memory of the joyful times we have together. The oil is our combined lubricant, the fish are your sperm, my throat is... I hope you like this. I like it very much.

She shut her eyes, and leaned back in her chair; and then without looking at what she had written, she continued:

Have you ever seen the film Hobson's Choice? I saw it with my parents when I was quite young. There are certain parts of it that stuck in my mind, and one of them is how the wedding ring that was used was a ring from the horse-brasses. This struck me as being so authentic. But I do like your idea of using a curtain ring.

By the way... so, you are busy at your computer? Too bad. I will come and cover up your screen with my skirt. It is quite wide, and will easily fit over both the monitor and your head. Then what will you be looking at?

She closed her pad and her eyes, and a fleeting image of Brian in his office, concentrating solely on his computer, flashed across her mind. She had always assumed that his concentration was because of his need to put energy into building up his business; but now she wasn't so sure. She would never know his intention at that time; but when she looked back, it could have been the start of his cutting off from her. What she was certain about was how she had felt then. Although she respected his need to concentrate on his work, she realised now that she had felt hurt by the way he seemed to isolate himself from her by relating solely to his computer when she called round on a Saturday in those last months. Perhaps if she had been less wrapped up in her thoughts about the loss of her parents, she would have been more aware of what was happening to Brian, and would have questioned him about his apparent detachment. But she had certainly been very wrapped up in the loss of her parents, and she hadn't thought to ask him much about anything. She had just wanted some warmth from him. And now she realised he had not given her the warmth she needed, and that she would never really know why that was.

She opened her pad again, and read through what she had written this evening. That's fine, she decided. She shut it, and put it back in its place at the bottom of the drawer.

That night she slept very well; and when she woke in the morning, she noticed that she felt a particular kind of deep relaxation that she had not known for a very long time.

46

It was about two weeks before she took out her pad again. She had felt no urgency to return to it. There had been plenty of times during the intervening period when she touched inside herself the knowledge of its existence. She knew it was there, waiting for her.

And now it was Friday evening once more. She was looking forward to meeting some of her friends the following day for a walk, followed by a meal. They were to gather at a car park. Curiously, it was the one where Tony had told her of his reunion with his wife Mary. This did not matter to her. That meeting was long ago, and she knew she would enjoy the stimulating conversation she could have with her friends. Tony was but a distant memory, and after all, he had barely been in her life. But what about the walk with him in the heather...? Well, there had possibly been something there, but it held no significance for her now.

Annette went to get her pad. She sat thinking for a little while before she began to write. She had started with a spring letter, and then two with summer dates. How about a date in September now? She liked that idea. Curled up in her chair in the middle of February, she wanted to create a September.

20 September
Dear Peter,

Thank you for your letter. Your 'negligence' is forgiven. I am a bit bemused by your great appreciation of my letters, but I am warmed and encouraged by it too. So, you would like me to write about a day we have spent together, enjoying ourselves. Here goes then...

It has been a lovely warm day. I have been out and have collected some blackberries. The sun was kissing me all over. I was wishing that a person had been kissing me all over too, and I wanted that person to be you. Then you appeared, as if from nowhere. The sun and the breeze kissed us both as we twined round each other amongst the birch trees. Slow intense twining, that gradually became more and more urgent. We knew now that we must go to a quiet room where we would not be disturbed. Soon it would be dusk, with beautiful colours in the sky; and then it would be dark and quiet outside.

Annette paused. She savoured the lovely images, feelings and sensations that she had conjured up for herself by what she had written. Then she continued...

We found that room, and I wanted to undress you, and you to undress me. But first we stood and kissed mouth to mouth, deeply, for a long time. Then gently we started to undo the buttons on each other's shirts, slid them off, and let them fall in untidy heaps on the floor. Then we held each other tightly with our bare skin meeting. You slowly undid my bra, and helped it down on to the shirt-heap, so that my breasts were free for you. You held them in your hands, feeling the weight of them, and tasting each nipple in turn. And now I could not wait any longer to put my cupped hand on your trousers to feel the shape of your penis and balls beneath. I needed to do this for a long, long time, to soak the shape of you into my hand.

After this we lay down side by side, arms round each other, holding each other tightly and kissing deeply. Time melted away into insignificance. You fed me with your saliva, and I fed you with mine. I felt your tongue grow hard and probe deeper into my mouth. My tongue responded in kind, and then we twined and danced our tongues together.

I could feel your hard penis pressing in your trousers onto me, and I became aware of my hunger for your naked parts. I was hungry for your smell and the taste of you.

I reached down and undid your trousers and slipped them off, while you moved your arms down me to remove my skirt and reveal my nakedness. The hunger of our kissing intensified, and I could feel your penis against my thigh. I reached down to hold your parts between my palms to absorb them into my hands.

Annette paused to consider. She wasn't entirely comfortable with using the word 'balls'. After all, her education in biology had named these parts as 'scrotum' and 'testes'. Brian had known these terms too, but he hadn't wanted to use them. She had slipped into using *his* word, not hers; and she had always used his word since, even in her own thoughts.

She went to her study, took the correcting pen she sometimes used, and neatly removed the word 'balls'. Letting the white correction fluid dry for a moment, she wrote 'testes'. That was better, *much* better. She was glad that she had never given in to his pressure to call his penis by any other name. As far as she was concerned, a penis was a penis, and that was that. At first, the other words he used had jarred on her, but then she had become used to them, and accepted that he wanted to use these just as much as she preferred to use her chosen term.

She returned to her writing.

We wanted our juices, and we each put our head to the genitals of the other, to suck and mouth and smell, impregnating the skin of our faces with the wetness; you with your hands on my breasts, and I with my hands on your testes, gently stroking and feeling and massaging and appreciating.

I wondered which of my orifices you wanted. We had a game. I focussed my mind on exactly what I wanted you to do, and we waited to discover if you could hear my thoughts. To which would you be drawn? Or perhaps you would want to sample each of them before making the final choice?

The sampling procedure began. First the mouth and throat. I licked you and dripped on you from my mouth, and I mouthed you and sucked you and thrust you deeply into my throat, again and again. I took each of your testes into my mouth through their wrinkly skin-sacks and rolled each with my tongue. I chewed your pubic hair. Then you sat naked on the side of the bed and I sat astride you, putting your penis deep inside my body. After that I lay, face down, still and compliant, to see if you wanted to enter me from behind.

The sampling was complete, and you had made your choice. You rolled me onto my back, gently thrusting at me, marking me with wet from your penis-tip. Then you sat astride me, and teased my clitoris with the head of your penis, until I writhed. You teased me more and more, smiling down straight into my eyes, so that we joined our gaze as intently as the coming together of our bodies. You had known my desires, as clearly as if I had spoken them.

I started to thrust at you with my pelvis, willing you to enter me. My mouth poured with saliva, and my vagina was awash with its juices. And then you were on me and in me; our mouths locked together, genitals fused, moving and pulsing as one. The rhythm of our movements was completely in harmony, intense but unhurried; and each of us was confident of the long slow path to the final crescendo.

We exploded in unison, crying out together, clutching each other ever more tightly, our shared wetness oozing from the place of our fusion.

As your penis furled itself into rest, we slumbered too, still wrapped in each other's arms. 'Love you', we whispered together.

Annette knew that there was something she had written that she didn't really like, but she had wanted to go with the flow of her writing, and nearly all of it had felt absolutely right. There was just one thing… She read through the letter from the beginning.

Ah, here it is, she said to herself; and picking up her correcting pen she removed 'Then I lay, face down, still and compliant, to see if you wanted to enter me from behind.' She removed the entire sentence with bold, confident strokes, and then reread the whole letter. Yes, it was fine. And there was one thing she was absolutely sure about – she wasn't going to lie on her face compliantly for anyone again! It hadn't been right for her at all. Brian had been so insistent, and she had been so willing to engage with him in the months after they had re-met, that she had gone beyond what was right for her. This was something that some people enjoyed. She knew that and accepted it. But she had never liked it, and wished that she had never agreed to it.

After all, she thought, in every facet of life, there are variations in what people want, and intimate relating is no exception. Just because your partner has an intense wish to do something with you, it does not mean that you have to comply, against your own inner wishes. What it does mean is that you have to respect the differences between one another, and find ways of talking about them sensitively, while enjoying the things you can truly share.

She shut her pad and went to her room to put it back in the chest. She felt content with what she had added to it this evening, and she knew she could return to it when she was ready.

Chapter Six

The following week she bumped into Mike in the corridor outside his office. She was on her way to photocopy some sheets for her next class, and her mind was on the problem of how many to get. She had just decided she needed ten extra sheets as spares, when Mike's door opened.

'Oh, hello, Annette,' he said, with a broad grin on his face. 'I'm glad I haven't had to come looking for you.'

Annette stopped, with a puzzled look on her face. 'What is it, Mike?' she asked.

'I wanted you to be one of the first to hear. I'm a grandad!'

'That's great, Mike. Is it a boy or a girl?' Annette knew that Mike's daughter, Carrie, was expecting a baby, but had not realised it was due so soon.

'It's a boy, and they're going to call him Michael, after me,' Mike said proudly. 'And by the way, you'll be invited to the christening. I'll let you know the date as soon as it's fixed.'

'Thanks. I'll look forward to that,' Annette replied. 'I'm sorry I can't stop to chat. I've got to get these copied.' She carried on down the corridor, while Mike went off in the opposite direction.

Time has certainly flown, she reflected, as she made her way to the photocopier. She thought back to the party when she had first met Carrie, and had the surprise meeting with Brian, and she tried to work out when that had been. After some deliberation, she decided it must have been around fifteen years ago. Fifteen years! So Carrie must be about twenty-eight now – around the age Annette herself had been at that party.

A baby... Her mind slipped back through the years to the night she had told Brian what she had been thinking, and he had seemed so pleased. She realised now that she had thought no more of having children once he had left her. A lump came into her throat, and she had to swallow several times to free it. She couldn't think any more about this now. She was at work, and had much to deal with, so she promised herself that she would take time this evening to look at her feelings.

It was six o'clock by the time she got home that day. She made something simple to eat, and then prepared to make herself comfortable in the sitting room. The central heating had warmed the room to a pleasant temperature, but she put the low flame of the gas fire on as well. She did not sit down straight away. Instead, she paced round the room in slow circles.

'I am forty-three years old,' she said aloud. 'I wanted to have a child with Brian, but that didn't work out. Then I forgot about intimacy, marriage, partnership, and children for me. Now I have started thinking about intimacy, and through my writing I am doing something to help myself. I hadn't realised until today that I had forgotten about having children.'

Annette began to cry. How could she have let that happen? But it *had* happened, and she couldn't turn the clock back. She was forty-three, and that could not be changed.

She tried to think about whether or not she would want a child, but she could not follow a coherent train of thought. In her distress, all she could think of was that such a decision would depend upon whom she was with and what kind of life they built together. Since she wasn't with anyone, it was a decision that she could not make.

Realising that it was impossible to sort this out in her mind immediately, she decided that it was a good thing she had even begun, but that it was best to leave it for now. She could return to it later.

She went to the bathroom, washed her face, and thought of the pad, waiting for her in the drawer. She collected it and returned to the sitting room, where she made herself comfortable and began to write.

14 October
Dear Peter,

Thank you for your letter. I'm glad you liked the story of the day we spent together.

You asked about the room we went to. I hadn't worked out where it was, so I am very glad to read of your idea. I do like your suggestion of the Lodge House. Already I have a plan of the inside of it in my mind. I'll describe some of it to you, and see if you approve. Of course it also has a garden, which is completely private as it is surrounded by a high stone wall.

Incidentally, you may not have realised that there is a railway station only two miles from the Lodge. From there it is quite easy to arrange for the local taxi service to take us. I think we can organise a fairly long lease, and the taxi-driver's wife might be willing to keep an eye on it for us, and keep it aired. It is good to have a local person to do that. Then we have the freedom to go there whenever we want, without much preparation.

The door into the Lodge is very thick and heavy. Fortunately the letter box is set into the garden wall just to the left of the Lodge itself, and this means there is no hole through the door. Inside the door is a small hallway with pegs for coats. Most of the ground floor is a single room. It has a large fireplace with a stack of logs at one end. The kitchen is a very small area at the opposite end of the room. The staircase is narrow and straight. There are thirteen rather steep steps up to the low-ceilinged landing from which the bathroom and bedroom are accessed. If you approve of this so far, please will you add your comments about the furniture and decoration. The only thing you have to remember is that the bed is near the window, so that from my side – the right, of course – I can see through it to the branches of the great beech and ash trees that are quite close by.

I should say that most of the garden is to the right of the Lodge (when we are standing facing the door from the outside). The stone wall around it is about seven or eight feet high. I haven't looked at the layout of the garden yet, but I believe there is a central area of grass. We could find out if the taxi driver would be willing to keep it cut for us through the summer.

Annette stopped writing for a moment, but continued almost immediately.

21 October
Dear Peter,
What joy! I see from your letter that you approve the Lodge without reservation.
Thank you for writing back so promptly. Never mind that you haven't yet had time to describe more of the interior for me. It is sufficient that you see the 'cosy Lodge room' in exactly the same way as I do, and you say we have the lease for five years! That is wonderful news. Already we are free to enjoy more of our time there. Here is a taste of things to come...
I am wandering in the fields and hedgerows – not too far from the Lodge. There are still some blackberries to be had, and I will gather some to supplement our evening meal. As I absorb myself in the task of collecting them, I am lost in the pleasure of exploring the undergrowth.
The many plants and mosses hidden there provide such a source of

fascination for me. I watch the busy spiders weaving their webs, and the beetles scuttling. Today, the leaves are half-changed into their wonderful golden colours, and the rain has stopped. I am picking in a very quiet place because I don't want to be disturbed.

Presently, my bag half full, I squat down to reach a particularly juicy-looking cluster of fruits; and just as I do so, I feel a hand come from behind me between my legs, and at the same time a gentle arm comes round my body to steady me. The stab of fear I first had melts away, because I recognise the familiar touch. The hand strokes me with its hard, man fingers.

I want to be laid down in the dry leaves under this huge ancient beech tree. Of course, I know that it is you who are with me – I can tell by your touch and the soft tones of your voice.

You have read my thoughts. 'The beech tree? No,' you say, 'we need to go somewhere warmer, and where we can be sure of no disturbance. We must go back to the Lodge.'

You grasp my hand firmly as we hurry along the track, and soon we are there. Oh, you had planned all of this! You have been here already today and made it warm for us, and then come to find me. I tug at your belt eagerly...

Annette hardly paused before beginning the next letter.

13 November
Dear Peter,

I got your letter safely with its enclosed plans. What an excellent idea to measure the rooms in the Lodge so you could draw up these plans. I see you have included the position of the furniture too. Of course we rarely bother with that large sofa in the downstairs room. The pile of rugs in front of the fire is where we usually relax.

And you have sent photographs of the old-fashioned bathroom furniture! That bath is <u>huge</u>, but it is of course exactly what we need. It is absolutely right for us – large and deep, with plenty of room for two. A heated towel rail? Excellent... we do need something to take the chill out of the air.

The evening before I got your letter you were in my mind a lot, and I wondered if there would be a letter from you in the post next morning. I wondered this because it has happened before – thinking of you in the evening, and then a letter arrives the following morning.

Yes, I'll remember that you are going to be away on business. One day I'll find a way of putting something interesting in your briefcase! It would amuse me greatly to think of you reaching into it for the papers for your meeting, and finding a token of our closeness.

By the way, you are right about the sense of taking some clothes down to the Lodge and leaving them there. A change of daytime clothes, a bathrobe each, and night clothes would suffice. We could do with some waterproof jackets and Wellington boots for outdoors. I'll put my mind to it.

Actually I saw recently rather a nice white cotton nightdress in a catalogue. I think I'll send away for one for a treat. It looks much the same style as that very old one I salvaged from my mother's possessions. When it arrives I'll take a photograph of it and send it to you. I have decided I want one anyway, so don't worry if you don't like it, I'll just keep it here and choose something else for the Lodge.

I want to start in the trees again. I can see some larch trees with their needles turning yellow, but there are plenty of broadleaved trees too. Those beech trees are really special, and we can usually find a dry patch underneath one of them. I feel my mouth grow wet at the thought. I am standing with my back to the trunk of a large beech tree. I feel your hands on my breasts – pressing them and caressing them, and feeling for my nipples through my clothes. You press your whole body on me, hard on the tree trunk. We kiss, the tips of our tongues dancing together. Hungry for you, I unzip and free you to reach out to me with our 'bridge'. I lift up my skirt and fit you into me so that we stand there, calmed and joined as we breathe in unison.

Oh I wish we were together like that now, it feels so right to be filled with your flesh.

My hands are clasped behind your neck, so I can feel the insides of my wrists on the bare flesh of your neck as we stand there joined. Wetter and wetter we become at the places of our connection. We do not want to move from this. We start to thrust to each other very gently, sometimes together, and sometimes taking it in turns. Our rhythm excites and soothes both at the same time. This is our slow, intricate, thrusting dance. The choreography directs us into small, circling motions at both places of joining. We pause only to loosen our clothing.

I whisper... 'Peter, I have to lie down now, I feel quite faint in the

55

intensity of our desire.'
Together we sink into the beautifully smelling crispy beech leaves that
carpet the ground.
  'Slowly Peter, very slowly please.'
  We are pressed tightly together, holding each other so closely in our
'merging dance', until you explode into my joyful response. And then we
lie, still joined, in our mutual exhaustion, until our bridge rests only upon
your body, where you will keep it safe for us.

Annette leaned back in her chair. She felt deeply relaxed. This had been a
very important evening for her. She had begun to face more of what she
had unconsciously denied herself – the possibility of having children. She
had also advanced her relationship with her paper lover.

Soon she would think again about pregnancy and a child, but not
tonight, it was too soon. She needed to give herself time. She would not
forget about it again, but neither would she push herself into thinking about
it too precipitately.

Satisfied with her progress, she closed her pad. She was aware of two
very important things that she had written. The first was the use of the
word 'circling', instead of the one Brian had used. She had never liked the
word he used, and she wished she had said something about it, instead of
wincing inwardly each time she heard him say it. The other thing was her
use of the word 'bridge'. She really liked that. She had never used it
before, and it sounded absolutely right. For a partnership such as she had
with Peter, 'bridge' was exactly the right word.

Chapter Seven

A few weeks later, Annette received the invitation through the post. The christening was to be in April, just after Easter. She wrote a note to Carrie, saying that she was looking forward to coming, and she put the date in her diary.

She wanted to think of something nice to give baby Michael on the day, and thought she would phone a friend of hers who was a glass engraver, to discuss what might be a suitable gift.

She had not written any of her special letters recently, but she had been thinking about babies. Something had occurred to her recently that was so obvious that she marvelled at how she had previously blotted it out of her consciousness. Her mother had been forty-five when she was born! How could she have forgotten this? But she had, until only very recently. So, although she herself was forty-three, there was still a little time left, should the circumstances be right, and she found she wanted a child. Feeling warmed by this realisation, she decided to have a quiet evening at the end of the week, and return to her special correspondence.

Friday came, and as before, she ate a simple meal, after which she moved to the sitting room with her pad. She did not delay, but opened it straight away and began to write.

9 December
Dear Peter,

I know you are still away, but I have a lot on my mind, so I am writing again now. This will mean that when you come back there will be two letters waiting for you.

The first thing I want to say is that I am hoping that there is a lake just through the trees, not far from the Lodge. We could take some warm clothes and something to sit on, and we could rest beside the lake and watch the birds. I am hoping there will be coots and moorhens and grebes. In the spring we will be able to watch all the baby birds. I like to see the baby grebes riding on their parents' backs. I could sit between your legs, and you could have your arms round me, and I will press myself hard against you and wriggle about from time to time, while we chat to each other about what we can see. You will be holding me and feeling me close.

We could sit like that for a long time, as we chat to each other about all the interesting things we are watching. It is very peaceful, and there is no one else about; there is no tension, and no disturbance. We know we can take all the time we want, and that when we are ready the Lodge is waiting for us; it won't ever go away. We sit until it is quite cold because we want to watch the beautiful colours of the sunset.

We are hungry now, and it is almost completely dark. We make our way back to the Lodge. When we are inside we turn the big key of the large metal lock, and you slide the huge bolt. We are safe and secure here – no one can intrude. We had laid the fire earlier, and now we light it. Soon there is a cheerful blaze. You look after it, adding small logs and pieces of coal. This provides much comfort to add to the warmth from the background heaters that we left on to keep the room warm and aired in these dark months.

I have brought some of our special foods – the special foods that we eat together. Today I have chosen the slipperiness of okra and of avocado pears. The texture of them in my mouth prepares my body to make its lubrication.

And now we lie naked in front of the fire, on the pile of warmed rugs. These rugs can absorb wetness, yet still feel warm, and we can wash them later if necessary, ready for our next joining. Today you will have to hold on for a long time we have decided. If I lie very still you think you will be all right. You insert yourself slowly and gently, and I hug you there. I have been practising every night, strengthening my muscles. My solitary efforts have not been wasted, because you exclaim at the improvement in the strength of my vaginal hug since last time! I will redouble my efforts when we are apart again. We lie very, very still... hugging.

But it is too exciting; you need to draw out, and we lie together, holding each other tightly while you quieten.

In that way, sure of our joining, we pleasure each other, while we are warmed in the firelight.

Relaxed, we chat about what we would like to do. Playfully, you tell me you think you can't restrain yourself much longer, you must have me. You want me to try to escape. I get up and start to run towards the stairs. You follow close behind, and I can feel your fingers brush my bare back. I reach the bottom of the stairs and start to go up them... one, two, three...

But you grab me back down and push me, very gently, on to the soft sofa, holding me there while I struggle and cry out in mock distress. You are always gentle, always careful in the intensity of our desire. We join together in our shared ecstasy.

Afterwards, we crawl side by side, exhausted and dripping, to our rug heap, and we doze in each other's arms...

And, next time, it will be <u>my</u> turn to chase <u>you</u>!

Annette had finished writing for this evening. She knew she did not need to read through what she had written. She remembered it all, and felt content.

Soon it would be the Easter break, and she would have time to think more about families, and children...

As before, she slept very well after her writing.

Annette saw Mike on the last day of term. Again, she happened to be passing his office on her way to the photocopier when he opened the door and appeared.

'Hello, Annette,' he said. 'How are you?'

'I'm fine thanks, Mike,' she replied. 'And I'm looking forward to the christening. I've ordered something up for baby Michael, but I'm not telling you what it is. I want to keep it a secret.'

'Okay, I won't press you,' said Mike, smiling.

She thought how well he looked. Being a grandfather seemed to have made him look younger. But then, he could not be particularly old yet, she thought. As far as she could remember, she had heard that he had married quite young, while he was still a student. Carrie's mother had found herself pregnant, and neither she, nor Mike, could even contemplate an abortion. They had married; and Carrie had been born a few months later. He must have been only twenty-one at the time. That would mean he was fifty-nine, or possibly sixty, now.

'I'll be forty-four very soon,' murmured Annette, as she continued along the corridor.

She had planned her Easter break well in advance. Two weeks were to be spent in Greece. She was travelling with a group of friends. They were sharing accommodation, but would split up according to their interests. She would spend some time enjoying the wild flowers. She had not been to Greece before, but had heard that spring was a lovely time.

On her return, she was going to spend a few days preparing for the summer term, and then she was going to Amy's for the weekend. Amy and Emma had promised her a surprise birthday treat. It was all very mysterious, and she was looking forward to it.

She would get back to her flat with a long weekend to spare before term started. It was then that she would have some quiet time to reflect.

Chapter Eight

The trip to Greece had been wonderful. Annette had several reels of film to be developed, and she had kept a journal as a reminder of the idyllic days she had enjoyed, sometimes in company and sometimes alone. The group had already arranged a reunion in four weeks' time, when they would pass photographs around and share their colourful memories.

Annette had next worked hard preparing for the following term, and after that had caught the train to London to stay with Joe, Amy and Emma. The birthday treat had turned out to be a series of treats. There were two trips to art exhibitions, and one to a concert of her favourite music. Emma, who had been learning to play the flute, gave her a brief recital of solo music, and Annette was very impressed. Before she left, they agreed dates in the summer break when they would come and stay with her. She intended to buy a sofa bed for the sitting room. She could sleep there, Joe and Amy could have her bed, and Emma could have the spare room.

As she sat on the train on the journey home, she felt very happy to have such good friends. When she got home, she must think more about her project. She had not mentioned it to Amy. Although Amy was a very close friend, Annette did not feel ready to tell *anyone* yet about what she had been writing in her special pad. And maybe she never would.

That evening found her sitting in front of the fire again. She would write more letters tonight, and then perhaps tomorrow she would be ready to do some more thinking.

9 January
Dear Peter,

Thank you for your letter, which arrived as soon as the post started up again. I am sorry to hear you have had flu. I have heard there is a lot of it about.

Now, I must put my mind to your request for a weekend at a small, cosy hotel. Perhaps we could have two weekends like that? Then we would have one to look forward to when we had finished the first. I think I would like to have one weekend somewhere in the Highlands, and the other could be at a seaside place. How about a hotel on Skye, not far from the Cuillins? I think there might be a small loch nearby where we should see the flowers of the bogbean, if we plan our trip for the spring. The evenings are so long and beautiful at that time of year, and there wouldn't be any midges to bother us. Let me know what you think. If you are in agreement with my idea of a seaside weekend as well, I'll leave it up to you to choose where to go. By the way, I recently heard of a lighthouse that has been converted to a hotel, and it does sound very interesting. I'd quite like to stay in a round room! I have some details here:

'The location is spectacular, being only a few yards from the sea. One can view a wonderful variety of wild birds including cormorants, guillemots, gannets, skuas, shags, petrels and fulmars, as well as an occasional seal and porpoise. There is an Iron Age fort on a rocky headland adjacent to the hotel.

'The hotel is situated in 20 acres, and the surrounding meadows are covered with wild flowers including stonecrop, harebell and rare orchids. The meadows are also home to wild deer and rabbits as well as our own Highland cattle and Herdwick sheep.

'The hotel has been carefully created and furnished with no expense spared in ensuring the comfort and well being of our guests.'

Write soon to tell me what you think.

13 January
Dear Peter,

The wind is whistling round the house, and I am thinking of us, snug in the Lodge House, listening to the sound of it together. It is dark outside, and cosy inside. The living room is lit by candles made from beeswax, and they leave a subtle but distinct scent in the air. The gentle movement of their light is quite hypnotic. We are listening to a Vivaldi violin concerto. It is the E flat major – RV 254. The slow movement is very intense as you know, and we always wrap ourselves closely round each other as we listen to the intertwining of the parts. It took us so long to find a CD of it, because it is rarely recorded. We have to listen through it twice.

Before long we will eat together – something slippery, oily, and slightly salty of course. To make a start, I put a little olive oil on my cheeks and smear it around, staring at you all the while. You come to me for a long, very close, kiss; and I feel your body pressing against mine, all the way down.

Steamed okra, suitably cooled and inserted into me makes a delightful hors d'oeuvres for you. You hide giant prawns behind your pubic hair. I have to seek them out. I anoint them from you, before devouring them.

As an interlude, we take it in turns to chase each other round the furniture. (Of course, I am squeaking in mock fear.) Exhausted, we sink into our rug heap, and you produce that bottle of maple syrup that you had thoughtfully secreted at the side of the logs. The intense sweetness of it must be reminding you of your very early days!

Plans are being made! Tomorrow we will go to the station and catch the train into town. We will sit side by side on the train. If we put our coats across our knees, we can hold hands privately. I like sitting beside you. I can feel your arm and your shoulder up against mine all the time. That is good.

When we get there we can look at the clothes shops. We don't need to buy anything; but if we see something we might enjoy at the Lodge, we might just get it. As you know, I don't buy clothes very often, but when I do, I want something of good quality. You might see things you would like me to try on, and I'll do that. There may be some clothes to consider wearing only in private – certain materials, certain fastenings, certain designs for ease (or difficulty) of access?

I think I want to find a loose dress in bright orange, red and yellow. That would be fun! It could have lots of folds in it; and if I were wearing it, it would take you ages to find out where I was inside it. Maybe there would be some interesting underwear! Maybe we could buy things to try out.

Actually, I am looking forward to the possibility of the whole afternoon being spent looking at clothes. And on the way back on the train I will be thinking all the while about being at the Lodge.

Did you ever see that film 'The English Patient'? If not, try to borrow a video of it, and watch – with special concentration – the scene where Fiennes rips off can't-remember-her-name's clothes to get at her. It is done to perfection. Perhaps one day we could have some old clothes, so it wouldn't matter that they got torn, and we could have some fun tearing them off each other! I think I'd like that. What do you think?

P.S. I knew you would like the lighthouse hotel. Let's book the room right at the top!

Annette put down her pen, but picked it up again almost straight away. One more, she said to herself. Yes, one more tonight. And she resumed her writing.

22 January
Dear Peter,

You said in your last letter that you had written two. Well, the second one arrived this morning, and I took it in my bag with me when I went to see the physiotherapist. I read it twice while I was waiting for my appointment. I am sure my cheeks must have looked rather pink when I went in. Since then my mind has been flooding with all the things we can do together soon.

I have been to M&S to look at the underwear, and I bought the enclosed item. Let me know what you think about the colour and style. On the way back home I just __had__ to stop at the supermarket to buy a very large pot of Tiger prawns!

It is so wonderful how the connection between us is expanding and deepening. The possibilities for us are endless.

A strange thing happened to me last week. I bought a ticket for a raffle and, much to my utter astonishment, I won something. You'll never guess what it was, so I'll have to tell you. It's a bottle of Bollinger – 1985, I think. Have you any ideas about what we might do with it?

By now it was midnight, and Annette was more than happy to get ready for bed. She was glad to feel so relaxed. She had had wonderful holidays over the last weeks, and now she was further advancing her project. She had the start of term to look forward to in a few days' time, and then it wouldn't be long before it was little Michael's christening. She had already collected the engraved tumbler she had ordered for him. It bore the date and time of his birth together with his name, under an engraving of a baby. She hoped that Carrie would like it.

Tomorrow she would try to think about the subject she had promised herself she would dwell on.

The following evening found her back in her chair with her pad, and soon she was writing the next letter. She hardly noticed the ease with which she took up her correspondence, as it had become so natural to her.

10 February

Dear Peter,

That's amazing! You mean I chose your favourite colour...!

It is so good to get your letter. The postman usually delivers here at around 8a.m. He is a very kind and helpful man – just like the taxi driver who takes us from the station to the Lodge.

You remind me that you are away a lot over the next few months, and that you will find it difficult to get the time and privacy you need to write your special letters to me. And you ask me again if I will write about a 'conception weekend' at the Lodge. Of course I will. Here it is... and you can carry it with you on your journeys.

For some time we have known, especially as our genital fluids mix, that we want to invite a new person into our lives, a person who has come from the fusion of your cells and mine. We have seen it in each other's eyes, and we have watched the knowledge of it form in our gaze. We have exchanged words that confirm it; and we have started to prepare. We have been taking my temperature every morning, and reading the thermometer together. You 'read' my vaginal mucus as often as you can, for we need to know as accurately as possible when I ovulate. For some months we have been nourishing our bodies with good, wholesome food. We have talked many times about when and where...

And now it is spring, our chosen time, long awaited with intense but calm anticipation. Part of our plan is that you are the one to choose our destination, the special place where the conception shall take place. I trust you completely, and I know that you will choose what is right for us and the creation of our child.

We know that next weekend is favourable – my cycle is at exactly the right stage. We will leave on Friday evening, and return on Monday morning, so we have three full nights and two whole days; and we shall not spend a moment away from each other. Our bodies must never be more than a few feet apart during this time of ultimate fusion.

It must not be a new and strange place, it has to be a place that has already absorbed our resonance. It has to be the Lodge. You knew that. We did not have to say it to each other.

Together we will look at the fresh bright green leaves unfurling out of the cigar buds of our beech trees. We can stroll unobserved until late in the evening. We will be able to join in the vegetation, in the bathroom, in the living room, and in our bedroom – our lovely bedroom, with the chintz-

curtained window that opens to let in the sound of the breeze moving through the trees.

It is nearly dark when we arrive; but we must stay outside for a while. I am very damp with anticipation of our coming together, and I have a deep desire to mark the trunk of the largest beech tree with my fluid. I lean my back up against it and you pull down my clothes to bare me, so I can bend over, my parts in contact with the trunk. The sensation of the smooth bark excites me. You help by standing in front of me so that I can clasp your hips to steady myself, and you reach and stroke between my legs to help my juices run.

Our first 'conception joining' cannot be slow; we are too eager, too hungry, for that. You lean me upright now against the tree, and pull up my clothes. The air is mild, and the mossy ground is soft and dry. We kick off our shoes, and you strip off your trousers and underwear so that I can caress you, knowing what you produce, and knowing how we need it in an extra-special way now. You loosen the buttons of my blouse, and my breasts hang unfettered. I wear no support tonight. Your juices are running freely, and I catch some in my fingers to lick while you taste from me. I catch some more, and more... to trail it slowly round my right cheek, across my lips and round my left cheek. I paint my face with you.

I feel your tongue dart between my lips, and dart again. Then we join, searching inside those warm mouth cavities. You press your body hard against mine, and together we help our 'bridge' into me. It feels as if my whole body is filled with the pressure of it high up inside me. We stand, as if frozen in our union, my body impaled on yours. We are suspended in time... Ten seconds or ten minutes? We have no way of knowing.

I squeeze your penis rhythmically with the strong walls of my vagina, and we move it in and out so slightly as to be almost imperceptible. In my state of ultimate arousal, I feel our bodies transform into that state of ecstasy that is known only to us. We call to each other... 'my love, my love' ... and our pulsing follows.

We feel dazed. We stagger into the Lodge, which the kind and thoughtful taxi-driver's wife has made sure is warm for us, and go straight up the steep stairs into the bathroom. Casting all our clothes into a heap, we fill the deep iron bath and climb in. We are supported and held by the warm water, so that we can sit and stroke each other's arms and murmur our thoughts to each other, and kiss and rub our cheeks together, and sit, forehead to forehead.

66

When the water cools, we take a towel to dry each other. Donning our bathrobes, we collect nibbles of food from downstairs – olives and grapes – and make our way to bed, where we collapse, exhausted, into deep but temporary slumber.

I am woken by the sensation of your hand between my thighs, and your face between my breasts, my nipples becoming alert to your presence. I have a sudden rush of desire and urgency. Peter, I want you <u>now</u>... come to me ...

When you are back from your travels and have the privacy to write to me again, I want you to tell me what happened next on our conception weekend. I look forward to it.

Annette knew that this was the first time she had attempted to write about the deliberate act of trying to conceive a child. She had not planned to write like this tonight, but she had obviously been ready to try, as what she had written had come to her with such ease. She leaned back in her chair with her eyes shut, savouring the feeling of having taken yet another step. She did not want to dwell on what she had written. She just wanted to know that in writing this letter, she had made a start on what she had promised herself she would think about. And now, she wanted to sit and enjoy this knowledge.

Some time passed before she opened her eyes once more. When she did, she turned to the next page of her pad, and began to write her next letter.

2 March
Dear Peter,

I know you are still away, but I am writing to you anyway. I am missing you even more than I thought I would. I wish we had carrier pigeons at our disposal. The best pigeon would always be able to search you out, and take a message to you from me. On the return journey he would bring back a hastily scribbled heart from you. Before you go away next time we must fix up a way of keeping in touch.

When we are together again I want you to stand in front of me, facing me, and I will hold the insides of my bare arms up to you, and you will stroke them a bit, and lick them a bit. Then you will get that special margarine we bought not long ago, and spread a thin layer of it on my inner wrists and down my inner arms – the soft, vulnerable parts. I will lick the margarine off in long, slow licks, and you will hold my hands and watch me. Then you will rub your stubble all over the places where it has been. Sometimes you press hard and prickle me, and sometimes you brush over, like a feather. You love me I know, and you will never hurt me. I am not afraid of you. You are safe.

Do you think you would like a change from maple syrup when we are next at the Lodge? I found some Greek honey in a shop today, where the bees suck from thyme and other herbs. I think I'll buy a jar and bring it with me on the train. I wish now that I had brought some back with me from holiday. I want you to try some. I think you'll like it. I'll put some on my nipples for you; it is too good for a knife or a spoon.

Annette stopped writing. She felt satisfied with what she had managed to do. She thought again about the conception letter of this evening. She knew it was only a very small part of the whole subject she was attempting to consider. This was a start, and she was truly content to leave it at that. She had never before embarked on an act of deliberate procreation.

She shut her pad. It did not take her long to get ready for bed, and she was soon asleep.

On the last evening of her break, she wrote one more letter. Before she began, she realised that this time she wanted to write something short and lighthearted. However, she also knew that whenever she began to write, things came from her pen that she could not have predicted. Not wanting to constrain herself in any way, she wrote with her usual freedom of style, interested to see what emerged.

14 March
Dear Peter,

I popped into an underwear shop today, and had a look around. There were some things there that might interest you, but I'll wait till you get back before I tell you about them.

I must tell you about an aubergine I ate today! I sliced it into the rest of the vegetables I was steaming, and it cooked to perfection. Its flesh had a wonderfully fresh taste, and the texture was what I can only describe as sublime – exactly the right slippery effect. Eating it was truly an orgasmic experience, especially when I was thinking of adding our special

68

'dressing'.

By the way, I do like the cartons of oat milk that have been standing for a long time. I pour away the thin milk from the top, and I am left with 'cream' at the bottom, which of course reminds me of you. I will bring some to the Lodge along with that honey. I want you to see some, and we can decide what to do with it together.

Reluctant to put her pad away, Annette allowed herself one more letter. Before she began, she thought how, since last writing, she had left the pad, waiting, on the small table by her chair. That felt like a step forward.

But with the start of term beginning tomorrow, she knew she would put it back tonight in the special place in her chest.

14 April
Dear Peter,

You're back! I'm so glad! I went downstairs this morning to find your letter waiting for me behind the front door. I read it straight away, before I started work. I want to tell you that it affects me very deeply. I so want to be by the lake with you... to be astride you, not moving, because we are one... and to feel the flow into me from the you-side of our shared body. And when you are giving me all the licking I yearn for – the warm wet presence of your mouth on my most tender places – I know once again the utter bliss of our physical union; and I reach out for your parts, to fill my hand with them, to feel myself absorbing their presence through my palm, with a sense of complete fulfilment.

You write giving me a clear description of how you want your mouth to enjoy me. I think that really we should place ourselves for ultimate mutual satisfaction. I believe the French describe the position as soixante-neuf.

I'll tell you a little about how my mouth will 'speak' to your penis. I hold its shaft in my right hand, and begin by giving the head little licks, tickling the edges of your foreskin with the vibrations of my tongue. Your slippery fluid will soon ooze forth for me to smear across my lips, and round and round my cheeks, my nose, my eyelids, and my forehead. Regularly I return your penis tip to my mouth, to tease it with my tongue. This will be the best way to 'milk' it. My mouth makes its secret foam to spread over your penis tip and down both sides of its shaft in confident rapid strokes. Once thus coated, my cheeks will slide up and down the

69

length of your shaft. The rhythm is quite slow at first, but once the pattern is established I will move more quickly, alternating between light and firm touch. All the while I can feel your face pressing between my legs, and your tongue dancing there, on me and in me, and your sucking at my lips and what lies between.

And then the bliss. My 'coming' against your face, and your own pulsing – flowing down my throat.

Can we go back to the Lodge now? I want to sleep this night twined round each other before our body has to continue life in its two parts.

It is good that we have devised our secret code. Now we can pass messages that no one else can understand. Here is mine to you...

XXXXXMUCHXXXXLOVEXXXXXXXXXXXXANDXXXXTHESEXX
XXXXXXXXXKISSESXXXXXXXXXFROMXXXXMEXXXXXTOXXX
XXYOUXXXX

Before she shut her pad, Annette noted with surprise the date she had written at the top of this last letter. April 14th! She went to her bag and took out her diary. Yes, she was right, the date of Michael's christening was the 22nd. What a coincidence that her letters to her paper lover, that she had started writing in November, although in the fantasy of it being May, had now caught up with the actual month of the year – just at the point where she was going to attend the christening of Mike's grandchild... She wondered fleetingly if there were some hidden reason for this, but gave it no further thought.

70

Chapter Nine

The day of the christening was full of sun and brightness. It was a perfect April day. The small churchyard was full of daffodils, narcissi and crocus flowers of all colours. It was a time of joy, and the sense of new life burgeoning.

There had been a large group of guests, which had swelled the normal congregation to the point where the pews were completely filled. Carrie and her husband Allan had invited everyone back to their home, where they had a buffet lunch set out in the conservatory at the back of the house.

Annette had smiled at Carrie's obvious pleasure when she saw the engraved glass.

'Oh, how wonderful!' she gasped. She turned to Allan and Mike. 'Look what Annette has got for Michael!'

Mike had looked at Annette with a warmth that clearly valued the thought and effort she had put into obtaining this gift for his grandson. And when the guests began to leave in the middle of the afternoon, he had approached her.

'Thank you so much,' he said sincerely. 'It was wonderful of you to get that gift for Michael, and ...' Here he stopped and cleared his throat. 'If you don't mind my saying it, you're looking lovely.'

'Thank you,' Annette replied. She took his hand briefly on her way out. 'I'm glad you all liked my idea.'

She went over to Carrie and Allan, who were trying to calm the now fractious Michael. 'I must go now. Thanks for inviting me,' she said smiling.

As she left, Mike followed her out into the front garden.

'Annette,' he said. 'Would you like to come out to dinner with me? I know of a nice place in the countryside. It's actually a converted farmhouse, and it has long had a good reputation for wholesome food.'

'Oh... Thanks Mike. What a lovely idea... Yes, I'd really like to do that.'

'How about next Saturday evening then? I could come round and pick you up. Shall we say about seven thirty?'

'That would be fine for me,' said Annette, her face radiant as she walked down the path to her car.

She drove home and changed out of the pale yellow suit she had bought specially for the occasion. How kind of Mike to invite her out. Already she was looking forward to it.

Now she must turn her mind to preparation for the week's classes, and she would leave some time in the late evening when she could write more of her letters.

She had been so engrossed in her work that it was very late by the time she collected her pad. Feeling satisfied with what she had prepared, she slipped easily into her private project.

'The second of May,' she murmured. 'That's amazing! This means I have lived through nearly a whole paper year already.'

2 May
Dear Peter,

I read your letter and felt very wet almost straight away.

I must ask you an important question. Are you able to leave your body? I got your letter on Thursday morning, and on Friday when I moved to get up out of bed, I discovered that my breasts were very tender. Perhaps you had been with me in the night?

You said in your letter that you are eager to have a more full description of my mouth on your penis, and I am glad to oblige...

You lie on your back with your knees apart, and I admire what lies between. I move forward to be there, burying my face in your scent while I chew your pubic hair. I nuzzle your penis, and allow time for growth to its full length, wet forming on its tip for me to taste. I stroke up and down its shaft with my cheeks – gently, tenderly. I close my eyelids and in turn rub your wet onto each. I rub each side of my nose up and down your shaft. I make it very wet with the special saliva that is pouring into my mouth. I make small mouthing and sucking movements on the head of your penis, and then I return to my stroking of your shaft with my face, and the nuzzling in your pubic hair and around your testicles. I use my neck – each side – to rub up and down your shaft, and your wet leaves trails. I gently and respectfully place each of my nostrils in turn at your tip. Time passes unnoticed as we lose ourselves in this nodding rhythm. Presently, we are both ready for me to take your penis into my mouth, and I start to suck – quite gently at first, then becoming stronger as I grasp your testicles in my hand and tenderly vibrate them in that very special way. My throat begins to crave your entry. I dive to force the head of your penis in as far as it will go. Momentarily it stops my breathing. I retreat a little to gasp air before I dive again. You are thrusting a little now, and I feel your urgency build. I lean back, and smile teasingly to your face, but I cannot stay away for long... and already I yearn for our next opportunity...

We must have some more time at the Lodge where we never have to be apart from each other. The Lodge... where we can touch each other, lick each other, and join with each other, whenever we want.

We might even sometimes be joined with each other when we are making food. For that we will need a special love-stool for me to stand on so that I am the right height. We can eat joined up too. You can sit on a chair and I will sit astride you, impaled. We would have arranged food on a table beside your chair, and then we can reach out for morsels to feed to each other.

XXXXXXLOVEXXXXXXXXXANDXXXXXXXLICKSXXXXXXXXXXX
XXXXXXXXXXXXXXXXXXTOXXXXXXXXXXXYOUXXXXXXXXXXX

2 June
Dear Peter,
It was so good to hear from you. I will write a proper reply soon.
You asked about lipstick. I have been to the chemist's shop. There was a surprisingly large range of colour there, and I enjoyed investigating. I was there for about half an hour! In the end I bought one called 'crazy plum', and I'll put a smear of it at the bottom of this letter for your comments.

5 June
Dear Peter,
I once read a book by 'La Lèche League' where it was claimed that in some cases a grandmother could breastfeed a baby if the mother was completely unable to for some reason. Apparently, if the baby was allowed to suck very frequently, it could stimulate milk production in the grandmother's breasts.

This leaves us with an interesting possibility. We know that breast milk tastes extremely sweet, but it is such a long time since I was a baby that I can't recall the experience. If my breasts produce a few drops for

73

you, we will find out just how sweet it tastes, and you can compare it with the maple syrup and the Greek honey. Perhaps the holiday we were thinking of would be the time to try. Perhaps we could go to the Lodge for a couple of weeks.

When I was out shopping this morning I found very large Tiger prawns. Of course I bought some. I had to eat them straight away, in the car park. I couldn't wait. You know why, don't you? No pubic hairs though. Perhaps I could use shredded lettuce, or alfalfa sprouts? We must go to the Lodge again soon.

11 June
Dear Peter,

Thank you for your very lovely letter. I am lost for words, because you 'speak' to me about all the things I want to do, and without my first having to explain them to you. You just 'know' them and write them down for me. You were so right about the last course of our meal – natural perfection.

Yes, when we go to the Lodge, we will spend some of the time reading together. I would sit with my book in one hand and your naked parts in the other. Whenever I feel the urge, I can lean across and suck and mouthe you gently. Bliss. And all the while I would know that you will confidently explore my body whenever you want.

Working in the kitchen, at the sink, is one of my favourite pastimes, but only if you are standing behind me of course. I can wriggle my hips from side to side, and then flex my lower back and thrust at you, where I would feel the ebb and flow of your arousal.

Oh yes… and the making of scones… I would make sure to include some of our juices in the mix. And all the while, you must definitely help yourself to my breasts whenever you want. I will wear only a loose shirt, left open all down the front for ease of access; and I will have our bottle of maple syrup handy.

We will eat joined as you describe. Whoever picks up food can put it in either mouth; and then, as you say, we can exchange food in our kisses. I have an interesting range of little movements I will employ to keep you erect inside me.

We must go to the Lodge often this summer. I want to grow some herbs there. I have a friend who is an organic gardener, and she sometimes waters her plants with a mixture containing her urine. She tells me that gardeners through the ages have employed this technique. We could fertilise our herbs like this to make them extra-nutritious, and we will grow even closer as we eat them together. Most of all I would like to grow sweet basil. What would your choice be? We might even be able to grow a few tomato plants – the bush kind with the small tomatoes that last for only one bite. What pleasure we would have feeding each other with these – carefully transferring them from mouth to mouth, and perhaps posting one or two inside me for you to eat before you fill me up with yourself.

I so look forward to being with you on that secluded grassy patch in our walled garden at the Lodge. We could roll about there together, gently warmed by the not-too-hot sun.

When we go upstairs at night, I want us to put some cushions on some of the steps. You can grab my ankle as I make my way upstairs, and roll me over on the cushions so that we can do some pleasing things. I want to, very much.

In our bedroom I lean, naked, out of the window, and you gently thrust at me from behind, holding my breasts with your arms round me as we watch the twilight sky, and smell the lovely late spring air.

We sleep the night twined round each other, each waking and sucking whatever and whenever we want.

XXXWHYXXXXXXXXAREXXXXXXXXXXYOUXXXXXXXXXNOTXXX
XXXXXXXXXXXXXXXXXXXXHEREXXXXXXXXINXXXXBODYXXXXX
XXX?XXXXXX

I am very unwilling to sign off...

27 June
Dear Peter,
Your letter was waiting for me when I got back from the long drive home from A...

I didn't read it straight away. I decided to unpack the car first, and tidy everything away. It was difficult; but I waited until I went to bed, and read it there.

I am glad you approve of 'crazy plum'. I thought you might, but I wasn't sure. It's fun, isn't it?

Ah, so it is you who comes into my bed at night. My nipples are not so sore these days, so they are obviously more used to the sucking. However, I often wake up aching all over, and I am glad to discover that this is due to your 'doing things' with me when I am asleep. It is good that you have mastered the art of astral travelling.

The restaurant. How did you know that this is dear to my heart? I should have known, because we are so telepathic about such things. You only missed one bit out, and that's how you collect something important from me to eat with your asparagus soup. I want some of yours too... remember? I do look forward to the next 'restaurant instalment' from you. 'To be continued', as they say – or even more excitingly, 'to be concluded'!

With reference to your letter of the 18th...

Dear Bird-of-the-Same-Feather, I am so happy we have found each other. I have a mischievous thought of reading a Very Serious book on tape, and sending it to you, saying it was the one I was reading when we were lying together. It might make you feel a little frustrated! Oh good, you grab me and force me down (both giggling).

'No, Peter, don't... ' I murmur seductively.

I will have to make a list of nipple anointings, so we can have them on hand – supplies always at the ready. Or perhaps we could deliberately run out and have to make a shopping trip? This would be excellent, especially around the supermarket shelves. I might feel you behind me as I bend over the freezer for some of my favourites – deep-frozen blueberries. I must think of a good way of sharing these with you. When I crush one in my bowl, the middle bit squashes out.

Answer to your coded message:

XXXXXXXXPETERXXXXDARLINGXXXXWITHXXGREATXXXXX
XXXXPLEASUREXXXXIXXXXWILLXXXXSLOWLYXXXXXANDX
XXXXXXXXXXXXXXXXXXXDELIBERATELYXXXXDOXXXWHATX
XYOUXXXXXXXXXXREQUESTXXXXXASXXXITXXXXXXXXISXX
XXMYXXXWISHXXALSOXX

11 July
Hello Peter, Dear Friend and Lover,

Thank you for your letter – it has just arrived. But I had some trouble reading it, because although it wasn't raining, the postman had somehow got it quite wet. In places it was so badly smudged that some words are totally lost, and others are quite difficult to read. I think I've worked out most of it okay now.

Ah, I was interested to read about your 'Auntie Maureen'. I have to say I don't like the fact that she told you it was 'right'. I am absolutely convinced that a young person should only be responded to about sexual matters, and not led. And it is so important that responses should be only the ones that are entirely appropriate. Such encounters as you describe can easily become abusive, because the dividing line is so fine.

Annette stopped writing quite suddenly. Why had she written about 'Auntie Maureen'? Who was she? But then she remembered that Brian had spoken on more that one occasion about an aunt of that name. He had never said anything sexual about her as far as she could remember. Had she picked up something from him about her without realising, and now it had come out in her writing? Unlikely, but not impossible, she thought. Her head seemed to whirl; and she felt quite unnerved by what had come out of her pen.

When her mind steadied a little, it occurred to her that if she had indeed picked up something through Brian's references to his contact with his aunt, there was a possibility that it might go some way to explaining the parts of him she had realised she felt uncomfortable about. But this whole subject was largely imponderable, especially in the total absence of any ongoing contact with Brian himself.

She thought about the whole project of her letters to her paper lover, and how she had gradually felt able to write completely spontaneously about intimate things. She knew this was having a beneficial effect on her. She could feel it, although she could not easily put into words exactly what it was. She knew that the main thing was she was entirely free to write whatever she wanted. Never mind if it did not always sound quite right. Some of that was left over from her relationship with Brian; and where she saw it, she could always use her handy correcting pen! There were other things that she realised were to do with earlier stages of her own developing thoughts; and she was happy to keep them in her letters, knowing that they were a part of her that she had needed to allow. She knew that as she matured, she would no longer have need of them.

It was good to sit here and organise some of these thoughts. She felt stronger for having done so. She was convinced that her writing was the right direction to take – for the foreseeable future at least. She knew there was more she could write, and there was more that she wanted to write, although she did not have a clear idea of it until she saw it on the page in front of her.

She went back to the half completed letter.

Peter, I knew you would like the supermarket shopping, and there's lots more fun can be had there. There's potential for hours of fun.

We haven't been to the cinema yet. Let's go soon. It doesn't matter what's on, we might not see much of it anyway! But if it's a good film, I will want to watch it...

How long before the scatter cushions arrive? Tell me when they come.

I'm so pleased you liked the rosemary. Don't hesitate to ask if you want some more – either the 'anointed' kind, or straight 'original flavour' for cooking. I have such a surfeit, and would be glad to send you a whole bunch if you want. I will be pruning it soon.

My (head) hair has got too long. I have pruned that, and enclose the surplus.

Very much love to you.

XXXXXXXXXXXXXXXXXXXXDEARXXXXXXXXXXXXXXXXXXXXX
XXXXXXXXXXXXXXXXXXXXXXXXXXXXXXXXXXXXXLOVEXXXX
XXXXXXXXXXXX

Annette had finished for the evening. She had stayed up later than she had intended, but she did not regret having done so. She shut her pad, put it away, and got ready for bed.

Chapter Ten

Saturday came, and Annette spent the day catching up with her shopping and cleaning. As she worked, she began to think what she might wear for her evening out with Mike.

Sitting having her lunchtime soup, she decided she would treat herself to a new dress. Why not? There was the whole afternoon left before Mike came to pick her up, and she could spend it looking round the clothes shops.

Soon afterwards, she was in the ladies section of a large department store. She enjoyed looking along the rails, but found nothing that she wanted to try on. Her next port of call was a small boutique, where she had previously found an unusual skirt that suited her well.

As she entered the shop, an assistant approached her straight away to offer her help. Pleased to have the attention of another woman, Annette explained that she was looking for something new for a dinner date, adding that she had decided to treat herself.

The assistant thought for a moment, and then decisively searched along a section of a rail on one wall of the shop, picked out three dresses and handed them to Annette.

'You might like to try these,' she said. 'The colours will certainly suit you, and I believe the styles will too, but that would be a very personal choice. Would you like to show me when you try them on? I'd be happy to give you my reaction.'

'Thank you,' replied Annette. 'I'd like that.' She disappeared into the changing room.

In the privacy of the cubicle, she studied the dresses, trying to decide which she would try on first. Drawn to the one in merging diagonal stripes of deep blues and purples, she slipped it on. It felt instantly comfortable as she zipped it up and straightened the panelled calf-length skirt. The scooped neck and loose three-quarter sleeves suited her well.

She drew back the curtain to find the assistant just outside, waiting for her.

'I don't usually use this word,' she said, 'but to be honest, I think you look stunning!'

'I don't think I need to try on the others,' said Annette decisively. 'I'll take this one.' She went back into the cubicle to change.

When she re-emerged, she found the assistant carefully folding the dress with layers of tissue paper, before sliding it into the kind of bag that was used to protect suits from creasing in transit.

'All part of the service,' she said cheerfully, as she handed the bag to Annette.

Annette had no worries about the price. Today she had not given herself a budget. She had wanted something really nice, and she had found it.

Back at her flat, she hung her dress up ready for the evening. She selected a pair of flattish navy shoes from the bottom of her wardrobe, together with a smallish handbag that matched. She would wear a full-length slip, and take her navy coat. She spent the rest of the day finalising her preparations for work the following week, as she was meeting friends for a walk on Sunday. Since the walk was to be followed by the holiday reunion gathering, she would not have much spare time.

At seven o'clock she put on her evening clothes and applied a little make-up. Before putting on her coat, she found the silver filigree brooch that had been her mother's, and pinned it on.

At seven thirty precisely, the buzzer went. She made her way quickly down the stairs, and climbed into the passenger seat of Mike's Volvo. He had his radio on, but as he reached across to switch it off, Annette said, 'I think I'd like to listen to this, if it's okay with you.'

'Yes, of course,' he replied, and drove off.

A guitar duo, she thought to herself. I really do like this music. Aloud she said, 'Classical guitar music is very pleasant to listen to on a car journey.'

'I think so too,' replied Mike. He turned on to a road leading out into the countryside, and then added, 'I used to have an acoustic guitar when I was younger.'

'Oh, I hadn't known that,' said Annette.

'It's not something I usually broadcast,' said Mike, laughing. 'I can't say I got to a high standard, but I did enjoy making my way through some of the slow movements of longer works.'

'It's a pity you don't have your instrument any more,' mused Annette. 'Why's that?'

'I would have asked you to play something for me,' she replied, almost to herself. 'By the way, how far are we going?'

'I think it's about another five miles. We should be there soon.'

The music on the radio finished, and a talk about standing stones came on. Mike reached over and switched it off. This time, Annette did not deter him. She did not want to think about standing stones at the moment. She wanted to think about the evening ahead. She hadn't asked Mike for the name of the place they were going to, but she had known by his description that it might well be the place where Brian had taken her – ten years ago – to tell her he was leaving. She wanted to be inwardly prepared in case it was.

Mike swung his car into a drive, and stopped it in the car park at the front of the converted farmhouse. It was still broad daylight, and quite different from the darkness of the evening Brian had brought her here, but it was definitely the same building.

He turned to her. 'Do you know this place at all?' he asked.

'Not well,' she replied. 'I have been here once before, many years ago, and under entirely different circumstances.'

Mike got out of the car, and quickly walked round to her side to open her door. This formal but pleasing action warmed her, and she thanked him.

They walked together through the front door of the building, and Annette noticed straight away that the reception desk was in a different place. Instead of being just on the right as they entered, it was now directly opposite the door.

'Mr and Mrs Cooper?' the receptionist asked.

'It's Mr Cooper with a very good friend and colleague,' replied Mike.

'Just a moment,' said the receptionist, and she pressed a buzzer. A young man arrived, who took their coats and showed them into the dining room.

The low-beamed ceiling of the room was just as Annette had remembered it. There were paintings around the walls, but she had a feeling they might be different from the ones that had been there before.

'Mike,' she said, 'once we know our table, I'd like to look at these paintings.'

'That's a good idea,' he agreed. 'I'd like that too.'

Their table was under the window; and from it they were able to look into the cottage-style garden beyond. Before they had time to turn to the paintings, the waiter brought the menu, and they studied it together.

'Spring vegetable soup,' Annette said. She noticed Mike was on the point of making the same choice. 'Followed by...'

Annette was undecided, but in the end chose the vegan dish of stuffed aubergine.

'How about you, Mike?' she asked, looking up at him.

'I think I'd like to try the aubergine too,' he mused. 'It looks different from the usual things.'

Having made a note of their orders, the waiter disappeared, leaving Annette and Mike free to examine the paintings. The dining room was nearly empty, and they had no difficulty navigating around the tables. Annette recognised the name and style of the local artist who had painted the scene she had bought some time ago.

'Look, Mike,' she said. 'Do you like this one? If so, I can show you some more of this person's work. I have a small painting of hers at home.'

'Thanks. I'd like to see it sometime,' he replied.

Some of the others were in the style of famous painters such as Constable, and the Dutch artist, Hobbema. Annette always loved their woodland scenes, and she found these pictures almost as pleasing. There were also two of farm animals, painted as so often seen in the nineteenth century, when the proportions of the beasts were not portrayed entirely accurately. Certain breeds could be of interest, since some were very rare.

They saw the waiter appear with their soup, and returned to their table. Annette noticed that there was a bush of rosemary directly under the window, and she noted that the warmth retained by the wall would help it to flourish.

'What a pleasant garden,' Mike remarked, as he looked across the lawn to the enclosing wall beyond.

'Yes, I like walled gardens,' replied Annette reflectively. 'Not only do they offer privacy and shelter, but also the walls provide an excellent support on which to train fruit trees. I see they have done that here, but it's too early in the season to be sure what the trees are.'

'We could ask about them before we leave,' said Mike.

'That's a good idea. Perhaps they use their own fruit in some of the recipes they prepare later in the season. We could ask about that too,' Annette said enthusiastically.

Mike and Annette agreed that the aubergine dish had been an excellent choice. They finished with a fruit compote, which the waiter assured them was from bottled and frozen fruit preserved from the garden the previous year.

'So that answered one of our questions,' said Mike, over coffee.

'And we can get the answer to the other on our way out, I'm sure,' said Annette.

Indeed it transpired that the receptionist was able to provide them with a leaflet about the produce that was used regularly from the garden. Annette thanked her, folded it up and put it in her bag, while Mike paid for their meal.

'Thank you so much for a lovely evening,' said Annette as they neared her flat. 'Perhaps you'd like to come round for lunch one day next month, and I'll show you that picture?'

'I'd like that very much,' Mike replied, as he dropped her off at the door which opened to the stairs to her flat.

It was late, and Annette decided to go straight to bed. She hung her new dress behind her bedroom door so that she could see it when she was lying in bed. She was so pleased with it. It had felt very comfortable.

The following morning she was up early to make her sandwiches. She was to start the walk alone, and meet up with the others at the stile about a mile further on, as they were approaching from another direction.

The walk took longer than they had anticipated, and Annette was not back in her flat until after six. She thought how sensible she had been to do her work preparation before she went out with Mike yesterday.

She was tired and relaxed. The day's walking had stretched her, and she felt her leg muscles a little stiff, but that did not bother her as she changed to go out again to meet the others for their evening meal. Before she left, she remembered to put in her bag many of the photographs she had taken on the Greek holiday.

The evening was a great success. She was pleased to pass her photographs round and to see many of those brought by the others, as well as exchanging stories of good times.

Although it was quite late by the time she returned home, she took out her special pad once more. She hung up her coat, and was soon settled in her armchair in the sitting room.

15 July
Dear Peter,

Woe! I decided to go for a walk in the local hills. You should have been there with me of course. I had gone about 50 yards past the visitor centre when I fell flat on my face. Dripping with blood from my hand and knee, and considerably bruised at several other points, I wondered whether to abort the trip. But I struggled on up to the clear water below the reservoir, and washed off the grit and grime. The air was so perfect for walking, I'm glad I didn't give up.

Annette laughed. This was something that had happened to her a year or so ago; and she liked the fact that she had wanted to tell her paper lover.

What next? she wondered, and then found herself writing once more.

27 July
Dearest Peter,

I got a letter from my GP this morning to say that my smear test is due. I don't much like being entered by a blunt instrument, but I'll just have to put up with it. When I have made the date for the appointment I'll let you know, and then you can come along in your thoughts.

I'm really glad you liked the hair I sent. As you know, my hair is usually tied back, but of course you can loosen it for me – under private, horizontal, circumstances. Then I could stroke you with it if you want. You could use my tresses instead of a fig leaf.

Sadly, my hair is not as long as Rapunzel's. If it were, I could hang it out of the window and you could climb up it. Perhaps when we are next at the Lodge, I could hang a rope ladder out of the bedroom window, and you could creep up it and 'surprise' me at the window, just when I am thinking of getting ready for bed!

Grazes are mending, bruises are taking a bit longer – especially my left knee, which is still quite sore.

I really like your 'dining out' sequel. It is excellent.

17 August
Dear Peter,

I seem to be sabotaging my body quite regularly these days. Out for a walk on Sunday in a forest on a hill (a walk I like). On a flat bit of ground, I suddenly went over on my ankle with an ominous ripping sound. The pain was so severe that I just lay and tried to do deep breathing for a while. Since then it has turned an interesting black colour, and the pain is subsiding. Hmm. On the good side, I have just expelled the last piece of gravel out of my hand that has been embedded there since that other fall.

Here, Annette remembered a day on the moors with Brian – the day when she had sprained her ankle, and hobbling back to the bus stop had been very painful. Brian had helped her by encouraging her to lean heavily on his shoulder, and she realised that even now she could appreciate that kind gesture. She was glad to remember something that she could value. There had been pain, yes; but the whole event had been uncomplicated, and it was a memory she could bring to mind without any difficult feelings. The colours that appeared on her ankle over the following days had certainly been remarkable!

She returned to her letter:

In the autumn we must take some rosemary to the Lodge, and plant it up against the wall where it will be sheltered. I love the smell of the crushed leaves.

30 August
Dear Peter,
I am in the middle of recording some of Pelleas et Mélisande so that I can listen to it in bed tonight. Thank you for letting me know about it. I can't make out the voice of the person you told me was singing in it, but I will bring the tape with me to the Lodge, and then we can listen to it there together.

Thank you for your special crinkly hair. I have your last two letters on my bed with me. I smile when I read them. The morning after the most recent one arrived, I woke from a dream where I had been aware of some wonderful sensations – from the most tender, prolonged, gentle, loving experience I could ever imagine. Any movements were minimal, but deeply sensual, in an indescribably beautiful and connecting way. You must have been in astral travel that night.

Your coded messages become more and more masterly!

Ankle is much improved, thank you.

I have bought a surprise for us to share. I will bring it to the Lodge with me when we are next there. It is a pair of white linen pillowcases trimmed with old-fashioned lace. We can use them at the Lodge, and then each of us will take one of them home. After a week, we will parcel them up with letters enclosed; and the postmen will ensure that we swop, so that I will lie on 'yours' and you on 'mine'.

8 September
Dear Peter,
  It is a lovely mild evening at the end of summer. We arrive at the Lodge in a hired car that we collected at Crewe station when we met from our respective trains.
  I so love the trees around our Lodge – that beech where we have played together, and all the others too – the aspen with its chattering leaves, the oaks, the larches, and the ash.
  I packed my new nightie, and we can have such fun working out how you can peel it off me... More of that later.
  We haven't eaten yet, so this leaves POSSIBILITIES. I <u>had</u> to bring some aubergines. I'll take my coat off straight away and get to work at the kitchen sink. You don't need any more of an invitation, do you? I thought not! I feel your warm breath on the back of my neck...
  But wait, what <u>are</u> you doing? I can't get the vegetables ready while you are stripping me naked on the hearthrug. Mmmm...
  Peter, you are my lovely familiar lover. We know each other's bodies so well. We delight in our closeness, and in our playing together.
  Do you like my new nightie? See, it is made of white cotton, with tucks and embroidered flowers on the front. It has long sleeves and a collar. When I have it on, it reaches almost to the ground. You can have lots of fun trying to find me in its folds, and working out how to peel it off me. I'll give you an essential clue – undo the buttons down the front, and then pull it off over my head. But this is only possible if you kiss me and fondle me very frequently during the removal process.
  In bed tonight, we shall once more accomplish our own specially choreographed dance.
  Later, exhausted, we'll doze off, side by side, entwined and merged in our delicious dampnesses. We stay as one through the night, and wake into a whole day together, before another night of union.
  ... dear Peter, I breathe in your scent and your essence.

XXXTHEXXXXTIMEXXXXXXDRAWSXXXXXNEARXXXXFORXX
XXAXXXXXXXXXXXXDEEPERXXXXXXXXXXXXXXCOMMUNIONX
XXXXXXXXXXX

25 September
My dearest,
I am delighted to hear that you are more than enthusiastic about my pillowcase idea.

At the weekend I was at a place that collects and sells 'architectural salvage'. There are old baths, washbasins, doors, panelling, doorknobs, fireplaces and many other items. It is fascinating to look around at everything. Upstairs I found an antique iron bedstead upon which was heaped a lot of old-fashioned bedding. Searching through it, I found a pair of pillowcases that will be ideal for our purpose, so of course I bought them straight away.

The most beautiful fireplace had decorative tiles on either side of it with rather lovely birds depicted on them. I wished we had that one at the Lodge.

How about drawing up a plan of its garden and its wall to show how there is that small patch to the rear, and the main part to the right? We'll include those trees to the left, just outside our boundary, at the start of the woodland where our special beech tree is located.

Ah, I am re-reading your comments on my nightie. From now on we have the new pastimes of 'rummaging' and 'lifting up'. Of course, the former should last for a good stretch of time, and even the latter could be prolonged. It would be such fun.

When we are at the Lodge again on a warm evening, I will put on my special nightie, and run out into the garden with bare feet. You can chase me (slowly) round the grass, and we will both be laughing. If you chase me slowly, I won't be frightened. After a while I'll let you catch me, and we can embrace passionately. I will pull up the sleeves of my nightie to bare my lower arms to feel you with and take you in. I'll rub my inner arms on your cheeks to feel your bristles. You want me to come back indoors. But I won't come in yet, because I want to be outside on the grass. You want me on our bed, but I want to tease you by playing outside in the garden. I pretend to do some weeding, and you sneak up behind me and rummage up my nightie. I like that so much.

About ten miles from where I live is a mansion house that was largely destroyed by fire during the war. It has an unremarkable lodge house – not anything like ours. However, it does have some very nice lakes. There are a number of waterfowl resident there, and a quiet boathouse. Yet more interesting, there is a little shelter-house made of stone and shells. It stands *at one end of a lake, and is truly a delight to see. In the woodland in the grounds is an icehouse. This conjures up fascinating pictures of life in the mansion before the days of electrically generated refrigeration. A part of the mansion that is being restored at the moment is lit only by candles and firelight. Consequently there are many dark corners – providing some unusual possibilities perhaps?*

And now, I have an impulse to curtsey impishly in front of you, saying 'My Lord', and you must bow low to me. I would look up and our eyes would join. My curtsey is part of our special dance. We know that.

2 October
Dear Peter,

I have your letter by fast postman today.

Your plan of the Lodge is perfect! I will put it in a frame and hang it up on the wall. Every night since we slept there with the pillowcases I have had mine on my pillow. It is nearly ready to send off to you. Remember to post yours to me the day after you get this letter; and with luck, they will cross in the post so that you will receive mine on the day I receive yours. There will be uniquely essenced pillowcases in transit.

Always remember when you come to me you must bring only your own scent – it must <u>never</u> be masked by artificial additions. And each time we are together, you must mark me with your special 'paint' that smells only of you, and I will do the same to you. My 'paint' says 'MINE – KEEP OFF'.

Aha! Not only have you instantly connected with the gardening game, but also you have embellished it most amazingly.

O Astral one, anoint my inner membranes, and feed from them whenever you desire. My body awaits your visitations. Today I bought some of the Agave syrup I saw in the local organic shop. I will cover my nipples one night to see how you like the taste.

You mention an intriguing folly. Please enlighten me further about it. I will eagerly await your reply. There was a significant folly in my childhood that we were allowed to play in and on, daringly and dangerously.

XXXXXXXXXTHEXXXXDARKNESSXXXXXOFXXXXXXXXTHEXXX
XXXXXXXXXXXXXXXXXXXNIGHTXXXXXXXXXXXXXXXDEEPENSXX
XXXXXXXXXXXXSOONXXXXXXXXXXXWEXXXXXXXXXWILLXXX
XXXXXXXBEXXXXXXXXJOINEDXXXXXASXXXXXXXXXONEXXX

XXXXXXAGAINXXXXXXXXXXFORXXXXXXXXTHATXXXXXXXX
XXXXXXXXXXXXXXIXXXXXXLONGXXXXXXXXXXXXMOSTXXX
XXEARNESTLYXXXXXXXXXXXXXXXXXXXXXXXXXXXXXXX

17 October

Dear Peter,

I was recently visiting a friend, and friends of hers came round with their 5 month-old baby girl asleep in her buggy. I sat with her in the bedroom, while the others chatted for a while in the living room. Suddenly her eyes opened, and I could observe on her face all the feeling states she experienced, one after the other. I could see what a huge task it was for her to mediate the experience of waking up in an unfamiliar place with a complete stranger, while she was in this entirely dependent state. I was fascinated to watch all the stages of this process. Some of them came, went, and then returned... before going away once more. There was 'This is all too big for me', and there was shock, confusion, and anxiety. All the while I spoke to her by naming each of the voices we could hear coming through from the front room.

After what seemed an age, her face softened and relaxed, and she sat there taking things in. All this time I reflected on how much a small person like this needs a secure, central 'buddy' (the 'mother person') to help to make sense of everything. I was affected quite profoundly to have the opportunity to observe this in such detail.

You asked me in your letter to write an account of the last night at the Lodge when I woke you up. Of course I will, but I'll post this letter now, and write it in another letter – all on its own.

Annette glanced at her watch. She had been so absorbed in her writing that she had completely lost track of time. It was nearly midnight already. Thinking of the busy week ahead, she knew she must put her pad away now, but she was also aware of a fragment of reluctance.

It's all right, she comforted herself. You can write again soon... But the feeling lingered. She went to her bag, took out her diary and consulted it. She had a meeting tomorrow evening until late, and the following evening she was giving a talk to the local historical society on pollen dating. Wednesday evening was clear though.

She made a note under Wednesday. It said 'evening – letters'. That felt good. It was the first time she had written anything to do with her plan anywhere other than in her pad. Yes, it deserved a place in her diary.

Her reluctance about relinquishing her pad had evaporated, and she made her way to bed.

Chapter Eleven

Annette's talk on pollen dating had been very well received, and the society had asked her if she would be willing to give another talk in the autumn. She had agreed to think of a suitable subject, and to write to them with her proposed title. She floated the idea of an evening in November, and made a provisional date, which she noted in her diary.

At last it was Wednesday evening, and she could return to her letters. This evening in May was still quite warm, so instead of sitting in front of the fire in her armchair she sat at the kitchen table. She looked at the date of her last letter... 17 October. It did not feel at all strange to be writing as if it were the autumn. In fact, it suited her fantasy well. She remembered how the dates on her letters had almost coincided with the date of baby Michael's christening, but apart from that they were always quite different from the day on which she wrote.

21 October
Dear Peter,

In the middle of the night you were lying sound asleep with your back towards me, and I was curled round you. I reached round and started to fondle your penis and testes – very slowly and gently. I could feel them moving a little as I handled them. I felt your penis stir, in small 'inflating' movements. It half grew, but was still quite floppy. I did not let go of it. I stroked the insides of the tops of your thighs. I could see you begin to wake, but you pretended you were still asleep. Your penis grew, and I began to rub up and down your shaft with the inside of my wrist, using your wet to help me to slide. I didn't wait long after that before...

Annette stopped writing, and sat gazing through the window at the sky as her mind ran on. She had no need to write down any more of what she knew in her imagination... and many minutes passed before she wanted to write anything more.

And now to my desire...

XXXONXXXXAXXXXXXXWARMXXXXXAUTUMNXXXXXXXXX
XXAFTERNOONXXXXXXBURYXXXXXXMEXXXXXUNDERXXXXX
XXXXXXXTHEXXXXFALLENXXXXXXBEECHXXXXLEAVESXXX
XXNAKEDXXXXXANDXXXXXRAVISHXXXXXXXXXXXXMEXXXX
XXTHEREXXXXXXXXXXXXXXXXXXXXXXXXXXXXXXXXX

3 November
Dear Peter,
    Thank you for your lilac-coloured letter. I'm glad you appreciated the
hairs on the pillowcase. I left them there deliberately of course. I did
manage to find one or two of yours when I examined your parcel that
crossed in the post, and I have the pillowcase on my bed.
    Thank you so much for the 'leaves adventure'. It is perfect. It is very
important to me to learn that the scent of leaves excites you in the same
way. Whenever I am out walking amongst fallen leaves I will think of you
and 'know' you again and again.
    Did I say earlier that I wore the nightie for a few nights, but not since
then? I often think of flitting round the grass of the garden of the Lodge in
it, and of playing the 'gardening game' with you.
    I want to play at 'mixing hairs' – beginning with head to head. There
are many other combinations that we must work through...
    And when you are lying on your front I will bite your buttocks – gnnn!
    Now for a very secret message:

XXXXXXLOCKXXXXXXXANDXXXXXXXKEYXXXXXXXXXXXXXX
XXXXYOUXXXXXXXXXXAREXXXXXXXXXCORRECTXXXXXXXXX
XXATXXXXXLASTXXXXXXXXXXAXXXXKEYXXXXXXTHATXX
XXXXXXXXXXXXXTRULYXXXXXXXXXXXXXXXXXXXXXFITSX
XXXXXXXXXXXXXXXXTHEXXXXXXXXWAITXXXXXXXXXXHASXX
XXBEENXXXLONGXXXX

13 November
Dear Peter,
    I have found some of that special invisible sellotape – just the same as
you use. I will put some on all my letters to you from now on. Nosey or
careless postpeople will be repelled.
    I enclose some wild rabbit fur I collected in the garden of the Lodge.
You will note that it is very soft. I have also a small grouse feather for you.

92

XXXDEARXXXXXXXXXFRIENDXXXXXXXXXANDXXXXXXXLOVERXX
XXXXXXXXXNEVERXXXXXXXXGOXXXXXXXAWAYXXXXFROMXX
XXXXMEXXXXXNOWXXXXXXTHATXXXXWEXXXXXXXXHAVEX
XXXBECOMEXXXXXXXXXXXXXXXSOXXXXXXXCLOSEXXXXXXXX
XXXXXXXXXXXXXXXXXXX

You are the key and I am the lock... we fit so well. When the right key is put into the right lock, it fits. The key must turn and the lock must open. Sometimes it springs open, sometimes it is eased open with much lubrication, and sometimes it smoothly opens and closes in synchrony with our special dance. Afterwards, it closes like petals closing for the night... but sometimes it still snaps shut.

Annette shivered. She closed her pad hurriedly, and went to put it away.

'I'll just put the heating on for half an hour before I go to bed,' she said aloud.

Chapter Twelve

By the middle of May, Annette had invited Mike to come for lunch the following Sunday. She planned to make a large salad so that there was no cooking to do, and there was no need to keep any food warm. She would also make a few small cakes the day before, and put them in a tin to keep them fresh.

She bought the extra food with her normal Saturday shopping. She did most of her preparations in the afternoon, and that left the evening in which to relax. The term had been quite hard, and she had recently spent long hours marking essays and test papers for several of her groups. She definitely felt in need of a quiet time.

When evening came, she settled herself in front of the TV to watch the DVD she had borrowed from the library. It was a recording showing many Venetian treasures, and she had been looking forward to seeing it.

However, after only a few minutes, she became aware that her mind had drifted away from the screen, and her ears made no sense of the sounds. What was affecting her? she wondered.

It was not long before she realised she was being driven by a strong feeling of urgency to write to Peter once more. She saw no need to resist her impulse. She could return to the DVD another evening. She stood up, switched it off, and went to get her pad.

Soon she was once more seated at the kitchen table, glad of the long hours of late daylight. She felt no need to write a date for this letter, and neither did she feel any need to address Peter by name. She wrote:

Your stubble will be just the right length by evening time. You can stubble me all over ...

Your plans for our second honeymoon are entirely agreeable to me. I have studied the brochure you sent of the hotel where we will be staying. I'll pack my special nightie. Write to me and tell me what else I must bring. This time we will most certainly conceive our child.

If I have my hair loose, it might get in the way of things we want to do. Sometimes we will have it loose, and sometimes we will tie it back.

I will wait to hear from you about what happened on the first day of our new honeymoon; and while I am waiting I will write about the second day. I will have it sealed and ready to post the moment the postperson comes with your letter.

****

The Second Day

It is the afternoon now. It is so lovely to know that we do not have to be parted at all – right through yesterday evening, the night, and now today, tonight, all day tomorrow, and the night after that. We have no anxiety... no need to think of how many hours we have left.

I tell you I want us to go out for a walk. We speak to the owner of the hotel and discover that there is an area of woodland quite close by that is full of interweaving pathways. He gives us directions and we set off. It is easy to find, and we are delighted to discover it contains many of our favourite trees. Most of the leaves have fallen of course, and there is that wonderful 'damp leaf' smell we both love so much. I point out the mosses and ferns to you as we walk along, arm in arm or hand in hand. We wander and chat until dusk, when we watch the light fading through the latticework of the tree branches. It is a clear night, and we are able to see the sky full of stars quite easily, until we near the lights of habitation.

The hotel has a snug sitting room with a log fire burning. It is so good to sit close up to each other, and watch the flames dance their random but determined darting dance. Our limbs lose any remaining tensions as the heat penetrates, and the flames' movements disentangle our minds. We sit like this for a long time. There is no need to talk; the flames are conversing for us.

As the evening progresses we are encouraged to eat. We smile knowingly to one another as we move to the dining room. We know that after a very leisurely meal we will leave this room for our room for the next stage of our joining – the invitation for our child to come to us.

Soup is served, made of locally grown vegetables. I think of having more, but you encourage me to join you as you make your way through the menu. Together we sample and explore. At last, replete, we signal to each other through our gaze, and leave.

Our room is heated to perfection – the ideal temperature for a naked person. We take it in turns to unbutton, unfasten and undress each other.

95

My jumper, then your jacket; my blouse, and then your shirt; my shoes, and then your shoes; my socks, and then your socks; my bra, and then you fondle my breasts and kiss my nipples; your trousers – I undo them v-e-r-y s-l-o-w-l-y, zip tooth by tooth. You hold my breasts, stroking my nipples as I proceed. My skirt... and you stroke my buttocks and thighs.

We shower together – soaping and rinsing each other, with kissings between operations – laughing happily. And when we are finished, we dry each other slowly and carefully, and clean our teeth together over the washbasin.

Now we are ready. Will it be a girl, or will it be a boy? This is not an important question. The issue of our bodies will be our new person, our child – and therein is the rightness.

We will play for a while; but when you come into me, it must be that I am lying on my back with you over me, deeply embedded.

We like to 'eat' each other – all over – small nibbles and gentle bites on limbs, torso and face. We chat as we move from place to place – a chatting of direction, appreciation, encouragement and knowingness. I bite one of your toes a little too hard, and you squeeze my hand in the special sign we have to alert me.

We stroke each other – all over – not missing anywhere. Sometimes I nibble and bite the parts to which I am attending. I like to eat your hair – your head hair, your beard hair, and your pubic hair. I chew and savour the textures. You stroke my head and face as I go.

You gently knead my breasts, and examine my nipples in preparation. Then you tongue them and squeeze them and suck them in all ways that we can devise.

In between we need very often to take each other in our arms and hold each other tightly, pressing ourselves together – knowingly but waiting.

Sometimes we lie quietly, side by side, holding hands, to calm any rising urgency. We have the rest of the evening, and all of the night.

Side by side, face to face, we put our palms together and gaze at one another; and then include the whole length of our wrists and forearms together.

I lie on you and you stretch out your limbs like a star; and I make my star to follow yours, our mouths meeting.

Love my mouth with yours. Take my face in your hands and love my mouth, dearest – my lips, my tongue, all round inside my mouth, and down into my throat.

Take in my saliva, and let me drink yours. We will share our other fluids when the time is right.

We are happy and joyful – hugging and caressing and stroking. We chat – there is so much to say – looking forward to the missed period, the pregnancy test, the whole pregnancy, and the birth. What names shall we choose? When will our young one smile, sit up, crawl, walk...?

Cuddling, stroking, murmuring – more and more we merge into each other – the meshing and merging of whom we are, into that which we become when we are as one. It is a physical and emotional union that is the nest in which our conception will take place. As our meshing proceeds to deeper levels, we begin to lose all knowledge of where one ends and the other begins.

We examine the fluids from your penis and my vagina. We feel the slipperiness of yours and each taste it, and then together taste it before loving mine in the same way. We nod to each other knowingly; these are the fluids that make our joining possible. Next, you reach high into me to collect some mucus straight from my cervix. Yes, it is the special conception kind – like the white of a new-laid hen's egg. This is the essential ingredient for your sperm to make their way into my womb. We have calculated well, so that we are together on exactly the right days.

Side by side and face to face we hold each other. I fit your penis-head to my clitoris, gently rubbing the two together, slipping and sliding on each other as you come to your full size and I become heated and swollen. Then we slide you into me, and hold each other tight and still for a while before thrusting a little, gently, and exactly in deliberate time with each other. Kissing, holding, clasping, gentle thrusting and murmuring, the pace and tension gather an imperceptibly escalating rhythm.

We both sense the moment at which we must rotate as one body, so that I am underneath in our continuing thrusts. There is a barely contained urgency now, and that determined milking action of my vagina is apparent to us both. All the 'kissing' is focussed in our genitals now... the mouths would distract. As you sense that your coming is not long away, you whisper to me, and my excitement intensifies and my thrusting slows. In the sureness of our connection I pull away a little further to make each thrust longer.

'Starting to come' you breathe, and I feel you begin – only a second before my own pulsing joins yours. With you deeply embedded in me, we clasp each other closely and lie as one, until long after our bridge slowly

returns to you.
At some time – not sure when – you lie next to me. We stay very close
all night. I have lain on my back for a long time to keep your fluid inside
me.

****

18 November
Dearest Peter,
    Your 'day 1' arrived safely, and was further proof that we are one,
heart and mind.
    All my love,

25 November
    I hope that you have received all my other postal communications, my
love. We have come together in a process which has infinite possibilities
now that I am awaiting a missed period. Remember to start counting the
days!

Annette shut her pad slowly and deliberately. She knew now why she had
not been able to concentrate on her DVD. There had been something far
more important to do this evening... She had not reread what she had
written, and she had not questioned her need to write it. Her need had been
obvious, and her writing was self-explanatory. She did not need to
consider what effect this area of her writing would have on her thinking,
and on the decisions she might take about her life, now or later.
    She quietly tidied her things away, and went to bed.

Mike pressed the buzzer just after one. Annette had finished her
preparations by half past twelve, and had been spending time looking out
some books that contained illustrations of interesting art works, which she
thought Mike might like to see.
    She pressed the button that released the street door, and waited at the
door of her flat while Mike came up the stairs. She could see he was
carrying a bunch of flowers.
    'Hello, Mike,' she said. 'I'm glad you could make it.'
    'Lovely to see you, my dear,' he replied. He handed her the flowers.
'Thank you, Mike. Do come in, and I'll find a vase for them. We'll eat in

the kitchen. I've opened the windows wide because it's such a pleasant day.'

Once in the kitchen she bent down and looked in the cupboard to the left of the cooker. 'Here we are,' she said, as she produced a medium-sized vase made of patterned greenish-coloured glass. She trimmed the flower stems at the sink. 'I do love these,' she said. 'Thank you so much, Mike.'

'I chose them because the purple colour reminded me of one of the colours in the dress you wore when we ate out together,' said Mike. 'To be honest, I was more interested in that than in the botanical name!'

'Oh, Mike!' exclaimed Annette, laughing.

When lunch was over, she led the way to her sitting room. 'Let's sit here for a while,' she said. 'I have some books that might interest you. Oh, I nearly forgot... I'll go and get the picture. It's hanging in my room. I won't be a moment.'

She soon returned, and handed the picture to Mike, who studied it closely.

'I can certainly see the similarity in style,' he mused, 'although the subject is quite different.' He scrutinised it again, and then added, 'Do you happen to know where the artist lives?'

'Not really,' replied Annette. 'But I can tell you where the small gallery is. They're sure to know.'

'Thanks. I'd appreciate that.'

'Are you thinking of buying something yourself?' asked Annette with interest.

'Er... yes... I think I am,' Mike admitted. 'Well... at least I'd like to think about it, and have a look at what might be available.'

Annette found the address of the gallery and wrote it down, together with directions of how to get there. Mike thanked her, and put the piece of paper in his jacket pocket. Turning to the pile of books to which Annette had directed him, he said, 'I see you have a book here like one I have at home.'

'Which is that?'

'It's this one about Van Gogh. It's one of my favourites.'

Time passed pleasantly as they studied Annette's books together, reading out passages of interest, and discussing aspects of the choice of colour and form by various artists.

Presently, Mike caught sight of the clock on the mantelshelf, and said,

'I see it's getting late. I hope I haven't overstayed my welcome?'

'No, of course you haven't,' replied Annette. 'I didn't need to keep an eye on the time particularly, but I think I ought to get on now with some reading I have to do. Thank you for coming round. I've really enjoyed your company.'

'Thank *you*,' said Mike. 'Would...' he faltered for a moment before going on. 'Would you like to come out for a walk sometime next month? June can be a particularly nice time of year.'

Annette noticed a tinge of anxiety in his tone, as if he were having to cope with some difficulty in making this invitation.

'That would be very nice,' she said firmly. 'Can I give you a ring in a couple of weeks, and we can fix something then?'

'I'll look forward to that,' said Mike, a hint of relief showing in his voice.

As he disappeared down the stairs, Annette called after him, 'Thanks again for the flowers...'

Chapter Thirteen

Annette had not written any of her letters for more than a week. In fact, although she never forgot about the existence of her pad, thoughts of it had not been in the forefront of her mind. When she considered this, she realised something new had happened. Snatches of the kind of thing she might write in the letters were frequently in her mind on a day-to-day basis, and she was attaching these thoughts less and less to her letters. She realised with a start that before she had begun her letters to Peter, she had rarely, if ever, had such thoughts in her mind for a very long time.

Now she was looking forward to phoning Mike to arrange that walk. In another week she would give him a ring. Perhaps she should think of a walk she might like to go on, in case he asked her if she had any particular ideas.

A few days later she felt again a strong urge to take out her pad. She knew that there were still some things she was trying to sort out through this 'correspondence', and felt that this might be a time when more would surface. Perhaps she could also write a few 'fun' letters. When she thought about all the letters she had written over the last months, she knew that most of them had had a very serious purpose, even though she had not fully realised it at the time. Even if some letters were written in a 'fun' way, they had an important significance.

She thought about how the 'code' had crept into her letters. Where it had come from she had no idea, but she had no doubt of its value. In the guise of that playful 'extra' privacy, one or two things had emerged that had surprised her.

She brought her pad to the kitchen table, and began to write.

1 December
Dear Peter,

I got your letter yesterday. I saved it up (as I usually do) until bedtime. It was so good to have it. I have missed you sorely since being with you over our conception weekend.

Thank you for the card you sent with the letter. I have put it up on the chest next to my bed, where I can see it as I lie.

Some news... Last week I decided to go to see two films, and also to a concert. I found pleasant company at each, which I appreciated very much. The concert was of guitar duets, and one of these was adapted from an arrangement by Bach of a Vivaldi concerto. Needless to say, the slow movement was exquisite, and definitely 'us'.

One of the films was called 'La Maladie de Sachs'. It was lovely in many ways, including the expression of sexual intimacy. Do try and see it. The short description reads as follows: 'A compassionate account of the daily life of a country doctor – Sachs – who has to face suffering, anxiety and the violence of human relationships; in short, everything that makes people ill. It shows Sachs's humanity and his rebellion against the arrogance of the medical establishment. The doctor really listens to his patients and takes notes. Writing is his therapy, or at least his analgesic. On meeting Pauline, he begins to see things differently... '

4 December
Dear Peter,

I had to write straight away. Guess what I found in an old suitcase that was stored in our boiler-house. There is a pink towel with lace added to it that almost exactly matches the lace on our pillowcases, and there is a lovely nightie in fine white cotton with delicate decorative needlework on the bodice, neck and sleeve ends. I will bring them with me when we next go to the Lodge, but meantime I will photograph them and send you copies of the prints. I am looking forward so much to wearing this nightie at the Lodge... it has plenty of scope for 'rummaging'.

Yesterday we had snow, and the hills are white. The roads are okay enough, but the gritting lorries are out.

My answer to your question is 'Yes!' I would most certainly like to be lying naked with you in our bed, with you behind me and me 'sitting on your lap', feeling your penis growing for us. I could reach between my legs and gently 'post' it into my vagina, then wriggle about and press myself down hard, so you are pushed high up into me. Once linked, we can relax and chat, and even doze a bit. If I feel your penis softening, I can do some more wriggling and pressing down to make it come alert again; or perhaps I would touch and fondle your testes (my mouth fills with wet as I write this). I would be able to feel some of our mixed lubrication too.

So now we would both be deeply relaxed. Of course it was stressful waiting to be entwined once more, and we needed time to thaw and melt before we could flow.

I'll have to turn round now so we can start our kissing and tonguing dance while I feel you all over with my hands and wrists and arms. It is so good to feel you again. I've missed you and missed you and missed you.

I have to go to the bathroom, and you chase me all the way there and all the way back. I tease you by bending down with my legs apart, but then I run away again, and you have to punish me by 'stubbling' my buttocks and giving them one or two bites (but not very hard).

Please note – I bought Tiger Prawns again this morning. I think you should therefore lie on your back on the bed, and I'll get the prawns and hide them in your hairy bits. After that we can ferret them out and eat them together – we bite from each end and meet in the middle. The joy of being together again!

Now you are on your back, and I sit astride you, sliding on you and leaving a wet trail to mark you as we chat about things we have done together, things we might do tonight, and things we are looking forward to...

I shall 'eat' you all over with many 'bites' that do not bruise or hurt – cheeks, arms, chest, thighs and abdomen. I am taking you in because you are mine.

No more playing and preparations now. I lie on my back, and you lie on me...

XXXXXDEARESTXXXXXXXONEXXXXXXXXXYOUXXXXMUSTXX
XXXXXXXXXXXXXXXXXXXFLYXXXXXXXTOXXXXXXXXMEXX
XXXXXXXXXXXXXXXXXXXXXXXXXXXXXXXTONIGHTXXXXX
XXXXXXXXXXXXXXXX

11 December
Dear Peter,

I have discovered a wonderful book that lists a large number of very good hotels. Each entry has a photograph and a description of the hotel with its environs, together with the scale of charges for the rooms. Guess where the book opened itself first! Yes, it was our honeymoon hotel, of course. I was just flipping through the pages, and the book seemed to decide to open there.

The next thing I want to tell you about is that I recently came across some hand-made chocolates of a rather unusual shape. They were oval, and were larger than one would normally expect. When I bit the end off one, it seemed as if it were filled with stiffened cream, not heavily sweetened. The experience stayed in my mind for a long time, and I eventually realised that it was _so_ like kissing mouth to mouth, with much saliva.

The weather here is very, very wet, and is not at all conducive to outside activities of the kind we enjoy.

I have found a large walled garden not far from here. In it is grown a wide variety of herbs and vegetables for the hotel to which it belongs. In better weather I am sure we could find ways of enjoying ourselves there!

I have a fantasy of growing a number of bushes of rosemary, harvesting soft new growth, and making a fragrant love-nest from them. I am sure you will approve.

20 December
Dear Peter,

On Friday I felt there was something going on at the back of my mind. Some time later I identified this as a sense of feeling sticky between my legs (although I wasn't), and I gradually recalled that I'd had a dream where I was lying on my back being entered. I remember being concerned about whether or not I was at a fertile time. It all seemed very real. Did you come that night?

Have you heard any of Arvo Pärt's music? I went to a concert to hear Vivaldi (our favourite), and the second half was Arvo Pärt's Tabula Rasa. It was _amazing_. Tell me what you think of it. Do you think it could be some more of _our_ music?

30 December
Dear Peter,

Thank you so much for your letter. It is tucked under my blankets, and I will read it again tonight.

Today I went for a walk to blow away cobwebs, but it turned out to be quite an adventure, because it involved much wading – through heather and bog. I had to grit my teeth and refuse to be beaten (although I was). In the end I pretended that I was David Balfour in R.L. Stevenson's 'Kidnapped'. That did the trick.

XXXXXXXPLEASEXXXXXXXXXCOMEXXXXXXXXXXTOXXXMEXX
XXXXXXXXXXXXXXXXXXXXXXXXXTONIGHTXXXMYXXXXXXXX
XXXXXBELOVEDXXXXIXXXXXXXXXWAITXXXXXXXXXFORXX
XXXXXYOUXXXXXXXANDXXXXXXXXXHAVEXXXXXXXXXXX
XXXXXXBEENXXXXXXXXXALONEXXXXXXTOOXXXXXXXXX
XXXXXXLONGXXXXX

12 January
Dear Peter,
   It was so good to get your letter. And you say you have plenty of free time ahead to spend spoiling me! This sounds wonderful, although I won't hold you to it if things intervene. It was a treat in itself to read what you wrote. Please feel free to sprinkle 'darling' as often as you want to. Such an endearment is always a pleasure to receive.
   The aftermath of flu has left me unable to walk very far, but very able to cough a lot. However, it is clear that plenty of the rest of the population are suffering likewise.
   Well, I am glad the thought occurred to you – 'Are we married in a way?' I must say that such questions occur to me too. I certainly don't feel like a mistress! Your suggestion of VSL (Very Special Love-makers) is more than acceptable to me. I now have an Arvo Pärt CD, and if I can find someone to tape it for me, I will send you some of the Tabula Rasa to listen to. I am not surprised you had not heard of him before. I certainly hadn't. I see that he was born in 1935. The programme notes further revealed: 'When his homeland of Estonia was part of the USSR, Pärt's music offended the authorities, and his Credo was banned by the Russian cultural police. This rejection forced him into a period of reflection and study of ancient music, which produced his current compositional concerns.' So now you know.
   I have made some progress with the homework assignment you set me on the subject of the 'Intruder'. It was tricky at first because I didn't want anything unpleasant. However, I found that I was able to devise an opening scene...
   I had to be sure I would know that the 'empty' Lodge contained the 'intruder' (alias you, my VSL). What came into my mind was that when I arrived at the Lodge, all was peaceful and quiet. As I went in, I noticed there was a trail of tiny pieces of quartz, arranged in arrow shapes pointing towards the living room. Then I am sure that although the Lodge

is OBVIOUSLY EMPTY, and I am ALONE, YOU are there – since these are the stones we gathered when walking in the Highlands last year. I followed the trail, knowing that it would lead to the 'intruder game'. You were waiting behind the door of the living room and you GRABBED me, slowly and gently, and I screamed in a pleased and happy voice. You were wearing your shirt OPEN. Lots of things happened after that...

19 January
Dear VSL alias My Key,
  Thank you for the number of things delivered by fast postman of late.
  I think I am beginning to get better. The act of staying vertical no longer takes all my energy. I even managed to go for a walk on Monday. I am definitely On the Mend.
  Here is a list of a few of my favourite things:
  The leaves adventure.
  The gardening game.
  The intruder game.
  Nightie rummaging.

13 February
Dear Peter,
  I have saved the red envelope as instructed. I will open it tomorrow – also as instructed.
  Thank you for your letter. I am very glad to read about the special penis brush, made out of my hair. I like that very much. No, I won't market my hair cuttings – all of them are for you.
  Already I have begun to deliberate about the next homework assignment you have set me – the Village Maiden.
  You will notice that I have a broad pelvis and strong thighs, so that I am obviously of peasant stock. Truth be told, my maternal grandmother was a farmer's daughter (actually, he had lots of daughters). Village Maiden insists that we bring some beech leaves into the cottage with us, together with some sweet-pea flowers from my little garden. These are the flowers I will twine into our love-making.
  Of course, now I know I will be visiting this place regularly, on my walks I am collecting stray feathers to put in my hair so my 'Game Keeper' can 'ensnare his prey' and take me to the cottage. (A touch of D.H. Lawrence, perhaps?)

I will be wearing a low-cut Village Maiden blouse, with my breasts held high so they can be seen easily from above.
A further thought... Afterwards, sticky and exhausted, we doze. As we start to stir we are feeling hungry. Any chance of some wild pigeon breasts, gently broiled over the remnants of the fire?

XXXXXXXXXXXXXXXXXXXXXXXXXXXXXXXXXXXXXXXXXXXXXXX
XXXXXXXXXXXXXXXXXXXXXXXXXXXXXXXXXXXXXXXXXXXXXXX
XXXXXXXXXX
(a very hidden message!)

17 February
    It is good to know that you like the Arvo Pärt music at least as much as I do. This means we are expanding our lives in more ways than one!
    This weekend we will both drive to Junctiontown Station and leave our cars in the well-supervised car park with no worries. Then we will catch the train together – heading for the Lodge. We can sit closely side by side for a couple of hours in the run-up to being alone together once more.
    There are not many people on the train, so it is easy to find seats where we are not directly observed, although there are other people in the carriage. Naturally we are holding hands. We have brought with us a few essentials. Much of what we need is always there ready for us at the Lodge, but we often think of other little additions to our repertoire of props for favoured or new activities.
    We sit chatting about things of mutual interest from the world outside the carriage, and things that have happened since we last met. We chat about things we would like to do, and things we have done before; but we dwell in the anticipation of what might next emerge. We have decided not to make any clear plan. The only important thing is that soon we will be in our own quiet spot, with unpressured time. We have no sense of urgency as we sit on the train, confident of our time together and our joint purpose, and joined under our coat.
    Our station looms, and I wake you up. The wan afternoon sun is surprisingly warm, and it kisses us as we step into the fresh air.
    As before, we take the local taxi. The driver knows us well by now, and he wishes us a 'good weekend', as we choose to set off to walk the last half mile to stretch our legs.
    I notice that the Dog's Mercury is beginning to appear at the sides of

the drive, and that the mosses have begun to take on that more intense green appearance of pre-spring. I stop to savour details. Although I still only recognise the more common ones, I plan to keep my microscope handy at home and study more of them, as I do want to know about the constituents of our 'bedding'.

There are two locks on the door. We each have both keys, but choose a lock each. This is a deeply intimate and significant act for us. Just inside, you close the door and lock it while I grab you, and pull you to me. We have all the time in the world to feast and feast and feast some more. Saliva... skin... warmth... stroking... sensing...

I open you up and set you free to stroke you with my hungry palms and wrists, pulling up my sleeves so I can feel you with my inner arms, and smear you thereon.

The trouble is my legs are so weak now that we must find a way to lie down, but we have to do this without losing our close contact – quite tricky, but not impossible... The taxi-man's wife had, as per our request, lit the fire for us earlier that afternoon, so the room is warm. Our special rugs are, as always, handily draped on the chairs. We draw them onto the floor to join us, and slide down onto them.

With time, all remaining tensions disperse, leaving us in a relaxed glow, and we roll onto our backs to chat for a while, still stroking. We talk of what we like and what we want; and we share guesses about what might emerge.

You have some ideas... You lay me on my back, while with long confident strokes you 'wash' my parts – your warm tongue and lip flesh on my 'lips'. You breathe into my passage, and taste its juices. Then you dance at its door, eliciting further delights. The 'decoration' above the entry place intrigues and fascinates you. You play, and nibble it to 'torture' me deliciously and interminably – our wish, and my utter delight. You 'know' to give me 'rests' and then more 'washing' in between. Sometimes you pull away and smile tantalisingly at me from above, before 'teasing' me some more. Sometimes you make 'saliva bubbles' and drip them in to aid your loving task. Sometimes you finger me, then 'look around' inside me to 'see' what is there. You know very well our desires, and you 'play' me beautifully, awaiting the moment when you move into irreversible determination in your quest of 'bringing' me to you.

The kind taxi-man's wife has thoughtfully placed a quilt within reach, and we draw it over us, and sleep in each other's arms.

XXXXXXXYOUXXXXXXAREXXXXMYXXXXXXXXXKEYXXXXXX
XXXXXXXXXXXXXXXXXXXXOXXXXXXXXXXXXXXBELOVEDXXX
XONEXXXXXXXX

11 March
Dear Peter,
I have your letter safely. I am glad you liked the box I sent you, and its
contents. It pleased me to construct it for you, and it pleases me even more
that you like it. Yes, you were right about the hair. There is plenty more
where that came from, so don't hesitate to ask whenever you fancy a fresh
sprig.
I see you have responded with great eagerness to my preferred mode
of train travel. Good. And I loved the things we did together in your letter
– glorious.
I see you have set me another assignment, and the scene that appears
in my mind is as follows:
You must take me to a restaurant, and order only slippery foods – as
wide a range as possible. If the restaurant cannot provide sufficient
variety, we make loud demands, *and, if necessary,* storm out *– having first*
arranged it with the proprietor. But as it happens, the place you have
chosen is ideal.
We have been shown to a narrow table, so it is easy to reach across
underneath it. Sitting opposite each other is the ideal positioning of
course.
The waiter provides some food-warming devices so that at no time do
we need to hurry. We want nothing so rigid as 'courses'. Spread around
us thus far are dishes of slightly-baked avocado pear, black olives, warmed
soft goat's cheese with garlic and herbs mixed in, softened butter...
(Please provide further suggestions...)
No cutlery – fingers only. Damp cloths are provided – bearing a
beautiful design of coloured flowers on white linen.
You dip your fingers into the foods, and very slowly and deliberately
smear the mixture onto your mouth (in which you have quietly secreted an
olive), while all the while our eyes are joined, and you lean over to 'kiss-
feed' me...
As you can imagine, there are too many variations on this theme for
me to write about here, and you will have to order another 'assignment' to
learn about them. But I could tell you a little about the slim spears of

chicken breast that we dip into mayonnaise before feeding them to each other...

By the way, there is one unbreakable rule in the above scenario – you are not allowed to do anything indiscreet while we are in the restaurant.

According to my instructions, you have arranged an en-suite room in the hotel next door. At eleven o'clock precisely, you guide me there, where we can wash and then collapse, exhausted, into bed.

XXXXOXXXXBELOVEDXXXXXONEXXXXXCOMEXXXXTOXXX
XMEXXXXXXXXXTONIGHTXXXXXSOXXXXXXXXXXWEXXXXXX
XXCANXXXXXXXXXXXXXXXXXXXXXXXXXXXXBECOMEXXXXXX
XXXXXXXXXXONEXXXAGAINXXXXXX

29 March
Dear Peter,

I have your two most recent letters, and have tucked them up in bed, ready for a few extra readings.

You mention the spring weather. Yes, things are indeed stirring. In particular, I like the quality of light at this time of year. It has a profound effect on me. I see several kinds of plant are beginning to stir again. I like the nip in the air. When June comes, the days will be so long that it will hardly get dark at night.

We can look forward to many happy weekends at the Lodge. Timeless pleasures. I am very pleased that you like my memory of the shared journey on the train.

I have recently bought a stick that I carry with me whenever I am out walking. I do dislike the tendency that dog-owners have to let their dogs run loose. I need the stick to prevent any sniffing. That territory belongs to you alone.

This will have to be a short letter, but I will write again very soon, my darling.

XXXMANYXXXXXXCLOSEXXXXXXXTIMESXXXXAREXXXXXXX
XXXXXXXXXXONXXXXXXXXXXTHEXXXXXXXXHORIZONXXX

Annette chuckled to herself. When she thought back through much of what she had written this evening, she saw it belonged to an earlier phase of her life. If she had been a bit freer in herself, and a fraction more confident about her intimate impulses, she would surely have had some of these images and fantasies before! It was not that she hadn't had any at all. But now she wanted to enjoy connecting with her spontaneity about intimacy, and revel in her newly discovered freedom – a freedom that allowed more to surface about herself than she had hitherto known.

She remembered the day when she had first written to Peter, her paper lover, and she could see that she had come a long way since then... a very long way. It was so satisfying to discover how she could connect with the person she had been, and also who she might have been, had not so many adverse events befallen her. At present, she felt no wish or impulse to enact many of the fantasy scenes about which she wrote, and she had a sense that there might never be any need. The act of writing about them was freeing in itself, and did not in her mind lead to plans that involved her current life.

Peter was her friend and lover... her very special lover... But Peter was her lover on paper – in her mind. Nowhere else.

Peter's presence had allowed her to be at any age or stage she felt drawn to, whether it were eighteen or thirty-eight, or anything in between. Peter's presence had allowed her to discover more of herself and to re-evoke what she had already enjoyed. Importantly it had allowed her to remember things she had felt uncomfortable about, and also to feel confident of where her boundaries lay. As time had gone on with her writing, she could detect any uneasiness more and more clearly. And she had most certainly benefited from the occasions when she had used her correcting pen to remove things she did not want!

She smiled at the memory of the rosemary bush she had seen under the window as she had dinner with Mike. How strange that she had seen this, just around the time when references to rosemary had begun to appear in her letters to Peter! Perhaps after all there might be some connection between her paper intimacy and closeness in her real life? But she discounted that idea, and reminded herself that rosemary was, after all, a very common herb, especially in old-fashioned gardens.

Mike... she knew she was looking forward to phoning him next week to fix that walk they had promised themselves. She put her pad away, and went to get some OS maps of the area.

Chapter Fourteen

'Hello, Mike. This is Annette speaking.'

'Yes, I recognise your voice, and I thought you might be phoning this evening,' Mike replied cheerfully.

Over the last week, Annette had been looking forward to this call more and more. She would see Mike at work and pass the time of day, but that was not the context for the conversation they were waiting to have, and neither of them would ever attempt to linger.

'I've been looking at some maps,' said Annette, 'and I've got a few ideas.'

'Good, I'd like to hear them. I've been doing the same thing, and we can compare notes.'

Annette read out her first suggestion.

'Oh, good thinking!' exclaimed Mike. 'I hadn't got that one.'

She read on.

'Very creative,' said Mike admiringly. 'Now, before we choose something, do you want to hear my list?'

'Of course,' replied Annette eagerly.

'My suggestions are for walks a bit further afield, actually,' said Mike. 'Here goes...' He listed three possibilities, each of which involved a full day.

'I hadn't realised you were thinking of a whole day when you suggested meeting,' said Annette, 'but that's fine by me, if we can find a free day in our diaries. I must say I like the idea of the second walk you'd thought of.'

'Me too,' replied Mike. 'I've got my diary here by the phone. Is yours handy?'

'Hang on a minute...' Annette went off in search of her diary, and was soon back at the phone, turning its pages. 'How about Sunday, the weekend after this coming one? That would bring us to the middle of June.'

'Ah... That's a pity... I've something on in the morning,' replied Mike. 'No... hang on... I think it's something I could change to the

Saturday. Leave it with me for now. Let's write in our walk for Sunday, and I'll get back to you to confirm it.'

'Okay,' replied Annette. 'I'll look forward to that. By the way, we'll need to think about what to do if it rains.'

'Yes, heavy rain wouldn't be too pleasant,' said Mike. 'And I certainly wouldn't like to give up our day just because of the weather. How about we each devise an alternative plan, and then toss a coin to decide which one to use in the case of a deluge!'

'Great,' said Annette. 'I agree.'

When she put down the phone, she felt different in some indefinable way. It wasn't a feeling of excitement, or of anticipation. What was it? After some consideration, the only word she could come up with was 'complete'. But what did that actually mean?

'More complete...' the words went round in her head in a pleasant and calm way. Ah! Now she had it. Why had she not grasped it straight away? It was not anything to do with what Mike had done or said, it was definitely to do with how she felt about herself – how she had experienced herself when talking to him, and now, afterwards. She knew she would be looking forward to seeing him on that day out; but more importantly, she was aware of a contentment inside herself that had nothing to do with whether or not she met Mike on that day. Her closer relationship with him was something that may or may not continue to build. And if it did develop further, then it was something that would be built on the relationship she had with *herself*. It was not something that could ever stand in place of that. It was not something that would cloud or obscure who she truly was. And it was not something that meant she no longer had to face things about herself, past, present or future.

Several days passed. Exams were mostly over now, and the stresses of the summer term were beginning to wind down. Mike had phoned briefly to confirm their walking date, and she was looking forward to it.

At this time of year, with the lighter evenings, Annette generally took a stroll quite late. She enjoyed these times. She usually went alone, but sometimes a friend or a neighbour would join her.

On this particular evening she was about to set off, but stopped at the door.

'No,' she said aloud, startling herself. I'd love to be out, she thought, but I know I want to get my pad out again tonight. There are things I want to write. She wrestled with herself. 'I could go out for a bit, and then write when I come back in,' she murmured. No, that wasn't right either.

She pondered for a few minutes, and then came upon a solution. The more she thought about it, the more appropriate it seemed. She would go out for a walk, and take her pad *with* her. She put it in her bag, and set off.

She was hardly out in the street before she knew exactly where to go. She would go to the seat... the wrought iron seat in the park. Not needing to think any further about her idea, she headed straight there.

It was a pleasant evening. The birdsong was in full concert as she strode along purposefully. She became engrossed in thoughts about the contents of her pad, so much so that she barely noticed the people she passed on the way.

Having reached the seat, she settled down and began to write.

6 April
Dear Peter,
  I will start with your most recent letter. Oh, I see you are missing me...
  Last night I woke up in the middle of the night, lying on my back, and with the bedclothes turned back. It was obviously *something to do with* you.
  Have you seen the film 'Being John Malkovitch'? If not, please do. I'd like to know what you make of it. I was very intrigued with the idea of the small wooden door behind the filing cabinet – the door that led to the portal...
  Now I'll begin to tell you a story and about a young woman called Verity. Verity was interested in agriculture, and she found herself a job for a year on a farm that had been recommended by the local agricultural college. She was about to leave school, and was due to start work straight after that. However, the farmer asked her if she could work there during the Easter holidays, as his wife had just miscarried twins and was not in a state to work. Verity found the farmer and his wife to be kind, and they were clearly appreciative of her help. She looked forward eagerly to moving in after she left school.
  Sad to say, when she did move in, the story became quite different. From the very first evening, the farmer draped his arm over her as they checked the animals together. She asked him to stop, but he ignored her requests, and his unpleasant and unwanted advances escalated day by

day...

Annette stopped writing. She could see that she was writing now about something that must have been troubling her for a long time. Some years ago the daughter of a friend had found herself in that situation, and had been deeply upset by it. Annette's friend had confided in her about it some months later. Annette remembered how she had felt great sympathy towards the young woman, and had wished she could offer more help than the support she gave.

It was now that she realised that she herself had been very disturbed by what she had heard, more than she had thought at the time. She knew this kind of thing was not uncommon – a fact that she found more than distasteful. But it was only now she had written about it that she could see something else. Behind her sympathy for the young woman, and her outrage that anyone could be harassed like that, she now knew that she had some feelings of her own that she needed to be more aware of.

Again she thought of Brian. Surely he had not harassed her? As teenagers they had been best friends; and when they met years later they became so close that they were planning their long-term future together.

Could it be that in her relationship with Brian she had felt some subtle, intangible, but consistent pressure to engage with him in ways that made her feel uncomfortable? This thought came into her mind as if from nowhere. But it linked with one or two other things that had emerged in her correspondence with Peter, her paper lover. Annette promised herself that she would bear this in mind, although she realised she may never come to any concrete conclusions.

Having thought it through a little, she felt able to continue her letter, and began to write again.

And you want me to 'take you in hand' occasionally? This is in interesting concept. My first image of how I would deal with you is to have you on all fours, with me standing behind you, banging a chair saying 'take that... and that... ', while you go 'ow... ow... ow', begging me to stop. Let me know what you think.

Yes, the taxi-man's wife is so helpful, isn't she?

And now to candlelight. Yes, let's have more of this. You will remember a long time ago I introduced you to beeswax candles. The aroma is so natural, and so subtle.

But this evening I have brought special candles – impregnated with a secret ingredient that will lull you into a sense of deep security in which I can tease you! When you are completely relaxed, and unable to resist, I produce a peacock's feather, and trail it across all the tickly bits of your body. I watch you squirm and writhe, begging me to stop. I do stop to give you little rests, but gleefully continue...

(I should impress upon you that a central rule of this game is that if you find it too stressful, you must say so, and I will stop immediately.)

Good night, dear one. It is late now. I will return to the other two letters of yours (not yet properly answered) another time.

XXXWEXXXXMUSTXXXHAVEXXXSOMEXXXXXLONGXXXXXX
XXXXEVENINGXXXXXXXXXXWALKSXXXXXINXXXXXVERYXX
XXQUIETXXXXPLACESXXXXXXXXXXXXXXXXXXXXXXXXXXXX

19 April
Dear Peter,

Thank you very much for your letter.

In answer to your question – no, that farmer did not get his way. As the story unfolds, you will see that he was crafty enough to want to elicit the word 'yes', so that he could not be accused of anything. All he got from Verity was silence. It is sad that she had to go through all that, alone, and could see no way out of it at the time. The whole story upsets me greatly.

We obviously have much more to enjoy around beeswax candles.

Thank you so much for meeting me once more at the beech tree – one of our very special places, Oh Very Special Lover.

3 May
Dear Peter,

Reading your letter is, as always, a breath of fresh air, richly scented with the natural aroma of leaves.

I hope by now that you have been to the post office to collect the delivery of photographs I sent.

You would have had quite a surprise when you opened the packet... Baths... My darling, I took these photographs especially for us. They show ten different old-fashioned baths from the architectural salvage yard I told you about. I have numbered them, and I want you to write out the numbers in order of preference. I hope you agree with my own choice. I will keep it secret until I hear from you. I am sure we are of one mind about this; and once it is established, we will arrange to have our choice installed at the Lodge. We will look forward to many happy returns to our haven.

The post-gardening activities that you outline in your letter are very acceptable to me. The weather will have to be a little warmer than it is now, but we don't have long to wait.

6 May
Dear Peter,

At last I have finished the other film. I know you have had to wait a very long time, but soon you will have the photographs of that Heirloom Nightie I told you about. I hope you are excited. I have arranged to get special permission to photograph those lakes I once told you about, and you can look forward to receiving these sometime in the next few weeks.

My rosemary bush here is flowering, so the ones at the Lodge will be too. I have been thinking... we should give the taxi-driver's wife a little more money for all the work she does to keep the Lodge at the ready for us.

I have put a check-list inside my special Lodge bag. I can't imagine ever forgetting anything, but it is good to have that reassurance.

I have recently discovered a new delight! It is a concoction of tofu, garlic, gherkins, and suchlike.

XXXXXSEEXXXXXYOUXXXXTONIGHTXXXXXXINXXXXMYXX
XXXXXXXXXXXXXXXXXXDREAMSXXXXXXXXXXXXXXXXXXX
XXXXXXXXXXXX

17 May
Dear Peter,

Thank you for your very-nice-indeed letter that I got this morning.

The leaves are coming out on the beech trees. We must go to the Lodge very soon. And I have a special request. When we are there, I want you to sing to me. Why on earth I haven't asked you before I don't know. I will feel the vibrations in your chest.

Medjool dates – have wrinkly skins – and remind me of...

As per your request, I give you a solemn promise that I will never bite any part of you too hard.

The rhododendron bushes are flowering.

Next time we go to the Lodge, you must bring some old clothes with you. I have already packed some of mine in my Lodge Bag. I expect you will guess what they are for... I want to try the 'ripping clothes off', because we haven't done that yet.

XXXXXXXXXXXXXXXCENSOREDXXXXXXXXXXXXXXXXXXXXXX
XXXXXXXXXXXXXXXXXXXXXXXXXXXXXXXXXXXXXXXXXXXX
XXXXXXXXXXX

20 May
Dear Peter,
I got your letter this morning. I heard the post arrive, and ran downstairs because I had a premonition that there would be a letter from you. There it was. I snatched it up and ran back up to bed with it.
This morning I reclaimed part of the vegetable patch in my garden. It had become very overgrown. After that I put three planks of wood, carefully placed, on which I can walk when planting and watering. I shall grow some <u>interesting</u> vegetables. I am <u>sure</u> you will approve.
I've read your letter several times already. It always delights me to read your side of our special conversation.
And my answer to your coded message is... I'll give it plenty of thought and consideration, because your idea sounds lovely!

28 May
Dear Peter,
I have your letter safely. Let's go to the Lodge very soon...
Today I smell like a chocolate cake. Someone recently told me that the skin on my legs was rather dry, and she recommended the use of a cream that has cocoa butter in it. It is all right to get whiffs of it, but the continuous smell is rather overwhelming. You might think differently. I'll bring it with me, and you can experiment with it.
I am so pleased you like the photos of the nightie. They are yours to keep.
And you approve the Medjool dates! I will bring some with me. We must get a large pot of Tiger Prawns on the way, O Mr Maple Syrup.
Meantime, don't think for a minute you are going to get anywhere near your computer to do some work – you haven't a chance.
P.S. I enclose a little of the cocoa butter leg cream so you can try it.

1 June
Dearest Peter,
Today I posted you a note to thank you for your letter. I thought I would not have time to write, but I do find I have a little after all. So here I am.
You have heard my deepest longing, and from the bottom of my heart I thank you.
I will see you very soon, my love.

12 June
Darling Peter,
When we parted, you earnestly requested that I write to you soon with an account of our days together. I have already made a start, and I enclose what I have written thus far.
As I drove to meet you at the station, my heart felt full of light and joy. Soon I would see you again, my VSL. You were at the station car park before me, and I could see you leaning against your car. You were scanning the road eagerly, hoping to be able to see me as soon as I approached. But I hadn't been able to tell you that I had a sudden problem with my car, and had to hire one at the last minute. You didn't see me until after I had parked. I saw your face light up the minute you caught sight of me.

Annette looked up from her writing. The light had begun to fade, and she felt a little cold. There were a few people passing through the park, and she assumed they were hurrying home.

She shut her pad, and sat for a while, thinking of Mike. She had known him as a colleague ever since she got her job at the college all those years ago. She had been pleased to be invited to the christening, and was surprised when Mike had invited her out to dinner as she left that gathering. That evening out together had been very pleasant, and had certainly been quite different from the one she had spent with Brian in the same dining room. Not only had she been with a pleasing companion, but also, she realised, she felt more complete in herself.

And now, she and Mike were soon to spend a day together.

She thought about how Brian had failed to turn up for what was going to be their last short meeting – at this very seat. Somehow it felt entirely right that she was sitting here now with her pad of letters to Peter, her paper lover.

She had no need to write any more at the moment, but she certainly felt the need to pass through the Garden of Remembrance on her way back home. She stood up, and directed her steps to the gate. Once through it, lines of her mother's favourite verses filled her mind as she passed where she had scattered her parents' ashes.

On the way home, she became aware that she had written in her pad for the last time. She knew she had no more need of her relationship with Peter. And when she was later putting the pad back in its place in the drawer under her father's scarf, she knew she would not need to keep it for much longer. There was no rush to decide what to do with it, and she felt confident that she would know when that time came. Meanwhile, the pad could stay here.

Chapter Fifteen

When Annette woke, early on Sunday morning, she could see immediately that the sky was overcast. She got out of bed and contemplated the drizzle. She had packed a small rucksack the night before, and had already included her cagoule and waterproof trousers. The weather forecast had been uncertain, and she had decided to prepare accordingly. Mike was to call round for her at about eight, and they could decide then whether to go ahead with their original plan or not.

The buzzer went at eight o'clock precisely, and she made her way down the stairs straight away. Mike was waiting in his car, and leaned across to open the passenger door.

'What do you think?' he said, nodding at the wet on the windscreen.

'To be honest, I'd like to stick to our plan, but if it's pouring down when we get to the start of the walk, we'd better find something else to do. Have you got your waterproofs?'

'Yes, I've packed them,' replied Mike, glancing over his shoulder at his rucksack that was lying on the back seat. 'I'm certainly willing to try for our walk, even if we get rained off when we arrive. Do you want to put your bag with mine? You'll have more room.'

Annette reached her bag over to the back, and Mike drove off.

'We should get there by about ten I should think,' he said.

The journey passed pleasantly. The conversation ranged from discussion about proposed changes at work, to politics, to art, and to colleagues.

About five miles from their destination, the cloud began to lift a little.

'I think it might be clearing,' said Annette.

'Fingers crossed,' Mike replied.

'It's not far now,' said Annette. 'And I'm definitely willing to put up with a bit of rain.'

'I like your determination,' said Mike, smiling. 'Let's give it a try. You never know, we might be lucky and find it clears completely.'

About ten minutes later, he drew up in the car park at the start of the route. There was only one other vehicle there. It was a dormobile, and its tiny curtains were drawn.

'I think they've been here for the night,' Mike remarked. 'Let's be kind and not slam our doors. Then they can sleep on.'

Soon they were striding down the path towards a ford across the river. Annette had thoughtfully brought her waterproof map cover, and had it hung round her neck for ease of reference.

'It might be quite quiet today,' she commented, as she waded carefully through the shallow water.

'It just depends,' replied Mike. 'Some groups of walkers aren't put off by anything!'

It was late afternoon by the time they reached the road that led back to where the car was parked.

'If it wasn't Sunday, we might have been able to get a bus back down to the car,' said Annette, who was limping slightly.

'Do you want to sit on the wall here, while I go down for the car?' Mike offered helpfully.

'That's really kind of you,' said Annette gratefully, 'but I think I'd rather keep moving. It'll stiffen up once I sit down. Since I'm slow, perhaps you could go on ahead.'

Mike lengthened his stride. 'I'll be back as soon as I can,' he called over his shoulder.

'Don't feel you have to rush. I'll be fine.'

Mike made his way back to his car as quickly as he could. Their day had been very pleasant. After the first couple of hours the cloud had lifted; the air had been exhilarating, and the views had been wonderful. What a shame that Annette had twisted her ankle on the way back down.

It was not long before he was driving back to pick her up. He drew alongside her, took her bag, and opened the door for her to get in.

'I'll take you down to the river,' he said.

Annette was a little surprised at this, but decided to go along with his suggestion. Once there, he helped her to a low section of the river bank, and removed her boot and sock.

'Put it in the water for a while,' he advised. 'It should help a bit with the swelling.'

'Thanks very much,' Annette replied, as she did as he suggested.

The effect of the cold water was very welcome, and Mike's companionship was equally so. He sat beside her and encouraged her to stay where she was for a while.

After this, he produced a bandage from his pocket.

'I always keep one in my pack,' he explained. 'You never know when it will come in handy!'

Annette was impressed, and was happy to allow Mike to bandage her ankle.

'I'll give you a hand back up to the car now,' he told her.

'That was a really good walk,' said Annette as Mike drove back. 'I enjoyed it immensely. It was an excellent idea of yours.'

'Not so excellent about your ankle though,' replied Mike.

'That'll be all right tomorrow, I'm sure,' Annette protested.

'I can't say I'm as sure as you are. I have an idea though. See what you think.'

'What's that?'

'Well...' Mike began. 'You live two floors up. It won't be all that easy for you to manage tonight and tomorrow at the very least. You could come back with me. I have a small guest room downstairs, and the shower room is next to it.'

'But I haven't got any other clothes with me!' Annette protested.

'Hang on a minute. I haven't finished,' Mike interrupted. 'I have a few of Carrie's things at home. I'm sure she wouldn't mind if you borrowed her spare set of night clothes.'

Annette thought for a moment. Her ankle was throbbing quite uncomfortably by now, and she knew there was some sense in what Mike was offering; but she didn't feel all right about borrowing Carrie's clothes without first asking her.

'Thanks very much,' she said. 'I'd like to take you up on that, but I can't agree to wearing Carrie's clothes unless we phone her first.'

'That's easy to arrange,' said Mike, smiling. 'He pulled in to the side of the road, took his mobile phone out of the glove compartment, and was soon speaking to his daughter.

'That's that fixed,' he said cheerfully as he put his phone back. 'We can wait and see what your ankle's like in the morning. If it's not too bad, we can set off for work early, and I'll take you round by your flat to get changed. If it's really painful, you can stay on at my house until I come back, then I'll take you home.'

Annette relaxed. It all seemed eminently sensible, and she felt she could accept Mike's help.

'I think I'll give in gracefully,' she said.

A couple of hours later, Mike pulled into his drive.

'Hang on. Let me get the door unlocked, and then I'll give you a hand in with your things,' he said.

After he had helped her out of the car and into the house, he showed her the spare room, gave her a towel, and indicated the door of the shower room.

'There's a seat in there,' he said. 'The dressing gown behind this door is Carrie's, and the rest of her things are in this chest of drawers. Take your time. I'll look for something quick we can have to eat.'

Annette slowly took her clothes off and slipped into the dressing gown. She found the shower easy with the help of the seat. When she had finished, she made her way into the dining area.

Mike was busy in the kitchen, but looked up when he realised she was there.

'I hope you like beans on toast,' he said, as he passed her a plate. 'Don't wait for me... just start eating. It's my mainstay when I'm short of time or energy. We can dig into the fruit bowl afterwards,' he added, pointing to the large bowl in the middle of the table.

'This is fine, thanks,' she replied as he handed her a knife and fork.

'I'll get you an extra pillow to put inside the bed,' he said thoughtfully. 'It'll keep some of the weight of the bedding off that ankle. By the way,' he went on, 'how tired are you? Would you like to watch a film or listen to some music before turning in?'

'I'm not too bad,' replied Annette. 'What films have you got?'

'I'll go through my collection with you when I've cleared the kitchen and put that pillow in your room. I won't be long.'

Not much later, Annette was sitting on a low chair in front of the TV, examining Mike's collection of videos and DVDs. It was not long before she noticed that he had several from an archive collection.

'Hobson's Choice!' she exclaimed. 'I haven't seen that since I was small. I saw it with my parents. Would you mind watching it tonight? I'd like to see that scene again with the huge spider climbing up the wall!'

Mike smiled, took the video, and inserted it in the player.

'Lights on or off?' he asked.

'I'd rather keep them on, thanks.'

By the time the film ended, Mike was dozing in his chair, and Annette wondered if he had missed much. It hardly mattered though, as he could easily watch it some other time. She did not like to disturb him, and made her way to the kitchen for a glass of water, wrote him a note, switched off the main light, and went to her room. As she was falling asleep, she thought she heard him quietly going up the stairs to bed.

She woke next morning to a knocking sound. She gradually remembered where she was, and realised that it was Mike coming to wake her.

'Hello!' she called. 'If you give me a minute, I'll get out of bed and see how I am.'

'Don't rush,' he called back. 'There's plenty of time. I set the clock early so we wouldn't feel pushed. I'll get some cereal. Come and join me when you're ready.'

Annette sat up, swung her legs over the side of the bed, and put her feet down carefully on the floor. So far, so good, she thought. She stood up, taking the weight on her undamaged ankle at first, then gradually putting more on the other. She reached for the dressing gown, and tried walking into the hallway. The movement didn't seem too bad, so she continued round to the kitchen.

'I think I'll manage,' she told Mike. 'Are you still willing to set off early?'

'Yes, of course. The only proviso is that you let me bring you back from work too, and see you safely home.'

'Thanks very much.'

True to his word, Mike helped her to her flat that morning, and ensured they both arrived at work in plenty of time. And he waited at the end of the day to take her back. Her ankle felt quite a bit easier by then, but she was pleased to have his kindness and companionship.

Having seen her through the door of her flat, Mike leaned forward and kissed her lightly on the cheek before saying, 'Goodbye for now. Perhaps we can meet up again sometime soon.'

She called after him down the stairs. 'Thanks for everything, Mike.'

Chapter Sixteen

The last days of the summer term passed relatively uneventfully. Such times were always busy, as they were full of students needing contact about a wide variety of problems, but there was nothing new or insurmountable in the difficulties they brought to her. Annette would be in her office for a week after the last students had gone, but it would be a time for quietly sorting through the backlog of paperwork that had inevitably built up of late.

She was looking forward to the long break from teaching this summer. There would, of course, be many things to arrange and prepare for the following autumn, but she could deal with them at a slower pace. She enjoyed organising events, study trips, and even timetables; but she disliked having to work against intense time pressures, under which she had little chance of savouring the pleasure she had in these tasks.

This summer, she had not planned a particular holiday away. Instead, she had arranged to visit a number of friends, each of whom lived too far away for a day trip. She looked forward to catching up with them, trying out new walks, and finding interesting activities to enjoy with them.

One day, after the end of term, when she was trying to reduce the height of the heap of correspondence in her in-tray, there was a light tap at the door, and she looked up to see Mike's head appear.

'Hello, there,' he said. 'Do you fancy a break from the mountains of paper? I'm just off to find some lunch.'

Annette glanced at the clock on the wall of her office. 'Goodness! Is it that time already?' she exclaimed. 'Hang on a minute... Let me put this in the right file, and then I can think.'

'Good, that's in the right place. Now... lunch... Where shall we go?'

'There's a café newly opened on that small side street just by the police station. We could try that,' Mike suggested.

'Okay. I'll join you in five minutes.'

Mike disappeared; and Annette put a few more papers away before going out into the corridor, where she found him waiting. They walked together out of the building, and into the sun.

126

The café was bright and cheerful. Mike and Annette chose a table at the door, and ordered bowls of gazpacho.

'This is just right,' enthused Annette. 'It's very handy for college, and this soup is perfect. Well done, Mike, for spotting it!'

'Well... actually... it was Carrie and Allan who found it last time they were staying with me,' Mike confessed. He seemed to be about to say something else, but must have thought better of it, and instead returned to his soup.

'How's little Michael coming along?' asked Annette.

Mike's face lit up. 'He's great... just great.'

'I'm glad to hear that. Do you see a lot of him?'

'Yes, I do. I usually see him every week, either at their house, or at mine. The journey only takes about half an hour if the roads are clear.'

Again, Mike seemed to be on the point of saying something else, but instead he broke a piece off his bread roll and studied it.

He's quieter than before, thought Annette, but this did not disturb her in any way. In fact, she had noticed that when she was with Mike she felt as comfortable with silence as she did with their conversations.

'Annette...' Mike began. But then he stopped. 'Annette...' he continued, 'I'd like us to spend more time together.'

Annette thought for a moment. 'I'd like that too, Mike,' she replied. 'We have a lot in common, and there are many things we can enjoy together.'

Although she had not been aware that Mike was particularly tense, she certainly noticed that he seemed to relax a little after that exchange.

'Shall we fix a time for another walk soon?' she suggested. 'I'm sure my ankle would be up to it, and I promise to be more careful! I'm away next week for a few days visiting friends. You don't happen to be free one day this weekend?'

'Actually, I'm free on Sunday,' said Mike, not attempting to conceal his eagerness. 'Let's try one of those other walks we had on the list we made last time.'

Late that evening, Annette could not settle. She had intended to read some more of a book she had begun the previous evening, but found herself reading the same paragraph several times. She could not work out exactly what was bothering her. She was satisfied that she was bringing her work up to date. She was looking forward to the walk with Mike at the weekend, and seeing her friends the following week. What could it be?

She paced round the flat feeling annoyed that she couldn't grasp what it was she needed to think about. Feeling cold, she put on the gas fire and drew her armchair towards it; and it was then that she realised what it was. The pad... her special pad! Her need to write the letters to Peter had passed some weeks ago, but the pad itself still existed, containing all she had written, and was still lying at the bottom of the drawer under her father's scarf. She went to get it.

As she carried it back to her chair, she knew that she was ready to think now about what to do with it. In fact, not only was she ready to think about it, she *needed* to think about it. She no longer wanted or needed to write letters to Peter, and now she also knew that she did not want or need to keep the pad and its contents any longer.

She sat with it on her lap, but did not open it. She had no need to. Some of what was contained in the letters was no longer of any consequence to her; and the meaning and purpose of the rest of what she had written had been retained inside her, where she had access to it wherever and whenever she wanted.

The pad itself was irrelevant now; but she had to decide what to do with it. As she sat and thought about this, she felt that it deserved a respectful and appropriate end to its existence.

At first her mind was blank. There seemed no easy and obvious route for its disposal. There were the office shredders at work, of course; but that did not seem right at all, and she discarded the idea as soon as it came into her mind. She knew of schemes for incinerating confidential material, but surely these were for large quantities of paper; and in any case she required something entirely personal. She had to admit that for now she was stumped.

But later an idea began to form in her mind. In about a month she would be seeing Amy, Joe and Emma. This time she wasn't going to their home in London. Instead, she was joining them at the cottage they had rented in North Wales for a week. She had contributed to the cost, and was going to be there for four days. It was a cottage Amy had used before, and Annette was sure she had mentioned there was an open fire in the sitting room, which they had enjoyed when they went during Emma's Easter holidays.

Annette got up and returned the pad to its drawer, quite clear now about what to do. She would take it with her when she went to the cottage, she would tell Amy how her writing had come about and how important it had been to her, and then they would burn it together on the fire. She was sure they could have part of an evening alone, as Joe was usually very accommodating to their need for a girls' chat.

Who knows... she reflected, some of the ash might go up the chimney and blow across the heather! And she chuckled to herself...

Chapter Seventeen

By mid-morning the following Sunday, Annette and Mike were striding along a ridge between two low hills. The day was warm and bright.

'Annette,' said Mike, 'there's something I'd like to tell you, something I want you to think about.'

'What is it, Mike?' she asked, as she noticed in the distance a hare had sensed their presence and was dashing out of sight.

'Annette, I have a lot of feelings of affection towards you, and I would like to think about considering a closer relationship than the one we already have.'

Annette was not entirely surprised. She knew that she had already sensed tones in his voice that indicated more than a pleasant companionship, but she had not yet considered any possible implications of that.

She walked on in silence for a few minutes, and then said, 'Thanks for telling me that, Mike. I'll certainly think about it. In any case, I'd like to say that I value very highly the friendship we have. We have known each other for a long time, although it hasn't been until recently that we've spent time alone together. But there is one thing I must ask you straight away.'

'What's that?'

'What about Carrie and her family? After all, you are her father, and the grandfather of her son. What would she think of my being more involved with you?'

'Actually, I'd thought about that, and I've spoken to her already, telling her how I feel, and that I was hoping to speak to you soon.'

'How did she respond?'

Mike laughed. 'She said she knew there had been a change in me, and she had already guessed why that was. She said she hoped that she would be seeing more of you!'

Satisfied with this information, Annette found herself more able to reflect on her own feelings. She had grown very used to living alone, and she liked her flat; but having a closer relationship with Mike did not have to mean that had to change. She knew she would like to continue sharing some of her life with him. Perhaps her feelings for him might deepen as they spent more time together.

On impulse, she reached out and took his hand as they walked.

'I've got quite a number of friends I'd like you to meet,' she said happily.

'So have I,' replied Mike warmly.